El Milagro and Other Stories

El Milagro

and Other Stories

Patricia Preciado Martin

The University of Arizona Press

Tucson

Second printing 1998
The University of Arizona Press   Copyright © 1996
Patricia Preciado Martin   All rights reserved

♾ This book is printed on acid-free, archival-quality paper.
Manufactured in the United States of America

01   00   99   98   6   5   4   3   2

Library of Congress Cataloging-in-Publication Data
Martin, Patricia Preciado.
      El milagro and other stories / Patricia Preciado Martin.
          p.   cm. — (Camino del sol)
      ISBN 0-8165-1547-6 (cloth : alk. paper). —
      ISBN 0-8165-1548-4 (paper : alk. paper)
          1. Mexican Americans — Arizona — Social life and
      customs — Fiction.   2. Mexican American women —
      Arizona — Social life and customs — Fiction.
      3. Arizona — Social life and customs — Fiction.
      I. Title.   II. Series.
      PS3563.A7272M55   1996
      813'.54 — dc20   95-32550
                                                      CIP

British Library Cataloguing-in-Publication Data
A catalogue record for this book is available from the
British Library.

Publication of this book is made possible in part by a grant
from the Arizona Commission on the Arts through appro-
priations from the Arizona State Legislature and grants from
the National Endowment for the Arts.

Dedicated

to my antepasados paternos —

My great-great-grandfather   José María Preciado

My great-grandfather   Juan Inés Preciado Ortiz

My grandfather   Cornelio Preciado Alba

My father   Alfredo Anselmo Preciado López

. . . in gratitude for my ranchera blood that instilled
in me a love for life, a passion for music and dance,
and, for better or worse, the tendency to shoot from
the hip.

And also to my hermanito,
Alfredo Preciado Romero.

¡Adelante!

Contents

Tejidos y Bordados

Needlework and Embroidery

In 1916, after years of painstaking needlework, Señora Gertrudis Bustamante Pacheco lovingly sewed the last stitch, embroidered the date and the last design, and tied the silken knot on
the crocheted border of her "crazy" quilt. She was a woman
who so loved her tejidos y bordados that, as one of her grand-
daughters recalls, she would arise at 5:00 every morning so
she could pursue her craft without neglecting her domestic
obligations.

I can imagine her, a regal and spiritual woman, stepping back
with satisfaction to admire her handiwork, crossing herself in
thanksgiving, and then gently folding the magnificent quilt on
her matrimonial bed.

The "crazy" quilt of Doña Gertrudis is a masterpiece. It hung
recently in a temporary exhibit of Mexican American pioneer
women's needlework and stitchery in a small historical museum
in downtown Tucson, where it drew exclamations of admira-

tion and wonder from the visitors who gazed on its intricate beauty. Doña Gertrudis Pacheco's quilt is a joyous kaleidoscope of her life: it is composed of more than six hundred swatches of satin fabric of various shapes and sizes sewn together in geometric patterns with her fine, precise stitches. The colors of the fabric are brilliant jewel tones — shades of blue, red, purple, pink, green, yellow, orange — and also paisley, white, black and brown. Each section is embroidered with a different motif of her design: native and exotic birds, animals, and flowers; dishes and household items; furniture (including a sewing machine and thimble); musical instruments; sports equipment; ranching artifacts; tools; and patriotic and religious symbols. In the upper left-hand corner she embroidered her nickname, "Tula" Pacheco, and in the upper right-hand corner, the name of her devoted husband, Jesús María Pacheco. The date of her wedding, November 22, 1900, appears in intricate stitches, as do the names and birthdates of her beloved sons, Arturo and Fernando. Upon close scrutiny, one discovers a remnant embroidered with the Spanish word "Recuerdos." Memories.

Gertrudis Bustamante Pacheco's quilt is a panorama of her life, celebrated in rainbow-colored swatches. In its exquisite presence, one feels her power and her message: her love for life, for her family, for the world of her garden, for her home, and for her altar. It is a journal that speaks to us more eloquently than words, a document as personal and biographical as a diary.

My mother, Aurelia Romero Preciado, was a literate and refined woman who instilled in me a love for words and a love for needlework: she taught me how to read; she taught me how to sew and embroider. I proved to be skilled at the former and, much to her dismay, clumsy at the latter. Only in the last few years, in my vocation as a writer and documentary historian of my Mexican American heritage, have I drawn a poetic and evocative analogy between the two disciplines. My mother would be pleased.

Just as Doña Gertrudis Pacheco documented the recuerdos of her life in a composition of multicolored satin remnants, I too have attempted, with these stories, to stitch together the kaleidoscopic swatches of my personal and collective memories, impressions, observations, visions, inspirations, and milagros. They are a verbal quilt of my mexicana life experiences sewn together with the fragile threads of love that have embroidered indelible images in my heart: my beautiful mother, Aurelia, bent in concentration over her treadle sewing machine; my abuelita Silviana striding through her garden to the chicken coop; my Tía Magdalena with her animal topiary garden; my father, Alfredo, puttering around our house with his endless chores; my sister, Elena, in her homecoming and wedding finery; the aromas of melting butter on still-warm, homemade tortillas and of simmering, herb-laced guisos and caldos that awaited us upon our arrival from school; a dance by the light of the Aravaipa moon; the somber abandoned ranchos and sad corrals of our forefathers; the humble barrios with their magnificent gardens, yard shrines, and altars; my great-grandmother Dolores' cracked coffee cup monogrammed with her name in gold letters; the framed cross-stitch samplers of my abuelita Mercedes; and most of all, the great heart and spirit of la gente méxico americana. The recuerdos are innumerable, and like Doña Gertrudis, I am sleepless.

My mother crocheted an afghan of multicolored, fine, woolen yarn the year I was born. It is faded and tattered now, and the passing of more than five decades has made the texture soft as silk. It is still an object of great nostalgia and comfort for me. I wrap it around my shoulders and my soul on the evenings that I wish to remember or dream. It is my hope that these cuentos serve the same purpose — a colcha of memories that proffers warmth and inspires visions of what is glorious and mundane, serious and humorous, earthly and spiritual, poignant and joyful, historical and magical, in Mexican American life and culture.

Acknowledgments

Quiero dar las gracias, como siempre, to my best friend and devoted husband, Jim, without whose love and financial support I could not have pursued my writing vocation. Gracias, también, to our children, Elenita and Jim, whose critical comments and literary advice I highly value. Mil gracias y cariño to my sister and brother-in-law, Elena and Diego Navarrette, and to my hermano, Alfredo, and his wife, Sue, who were the patient audiences for the first readings of many of my stories. I will always be indebted to Dr. Ana Perches of the University of Arizona Spanish Department, who invited me to speak to her classes and who embraced me and my work. Thanks to Susanna de la Peña, scholar and educator, who offered me friendship and a forum for my ideas. Estoy agradecida a mis editoras at the University of Arizona Press — to Joanne O'Hare for her directness and intellectual integrity and to Judith Wesley Allen for her gentle persuasion. Gracias to Chris Stuetz, who prepared the final manuscript on his word processor with accuracy and efficiency. And gracias, cariño, y oraciones for all my ascendientes and to all la gente linda I have met on my sojourns who have inspired me to write these stories.

El Milagro and Other Stories

El Milagro

The Miracle

I could have told you that something out of the ordinary was going to happen in Barrio Anita that summer. Everything seemed milagroso: the way the light glanced off the faces of the people so that you saw your reflection in their cheeks; the way the dust motes twirled and eddied and settled like golden powder in the narrow streets; the way the leaves in the cottonwoods trembled and burned like green flames and lit up the lampless alleyways at night.

And who could explain the way the air moved? There was always a breeze, even in the doldrums of July. And those brisitas, sweet with the fragrance of carnations, spilling out of rusty tin cans, down windowsills, up walls, and across driveways — cut back every evening into enormous bouquets that perfumed the home altars in the humble adobe houses, only to reappear in the same abundance the next morning.

My abuelita's neighbor, Doña Hermela, grew tomatoes the

size of pumpkins, and la Viuda Elías grew a squash so large it took her brother-in-law a whole morning to cut it up. Everyone for two blocks around had calabacitas con queso for dinner that night. And that's to say nothing of the chiles that grew in everyone's garden: one relleno was enough to feed four people! My Tata's cornstalks grew so tall and so broad that he set up a little stand and started charging everyone twenty-five cents to climb them, swearing on the cart of San Isidro that you could see the Río Santa Cruz from the top.

"Flaco" Miranda's cantankerous mule (never mind that the zoning commission hadn't allowed hoofed animals or barnyard fowl in the Tucson city limits since the forties) knelt down and let all the neighborhood buquis[1] ride him and swing on his tail without once showing his teeth. El Diablo, the aptly named one-eyed rooster in my abuelita's chicken coop, clucked like a Rhode Island Red and lay on all the eggs in the henhouse to keep them warm. My Nina's canary, Pedro Infante, sang "Barca de Oro" from beginning to end one morning and so startled my Nino that he set himself to whitewashing the house without even having to be asked.

My Tío Lalo, "El Rey de la Bacanora," excavated all the home brew that he had been stashing beneath the higuera[2] and handed it all out one Friday evening. He started accompanying my Tía Veva on her nightly novenas for the sick, the dying, the dead, and the resurrected.

[1] kids; brats

[2] fig tree

4

Lest you think that things were getting a bit too serious, believe me when I tell you that homely Lupita, who hid behind her mantilla and missal at daily mass and spoke only when spoken to (and only Padre Nuestros at that), bought a red dress, put a rose in her hair, and became the belle of the Del Río Ballroom at the Sunday tardeadas,[3] where one afternoon she won the "Grito"[4] championship away from "El Güero" Lionel and ran away with the bandleader to Los Angeles.

Anyway, the word got out, traveling like a dust devil through the alleyways of Barrio Anita. Everyone was talking about it: Sábado a las siete en la casa de Señora Sánchez.[5] No one stopped to inquire what or why, they just set themselves to polishing boots or shining patent-leather shoes, brushing the lint off their Sunday best sombreros, and putting their jackets and cloth coats out to air. Clouds of steam rose out of the windows of the houses all through the neighborhood as the housewives took to washing and boiling and bleaching and blueing and starching and ironing white shirts and dresses and blouses and petticoats and socks until they were as unblemished as newly confessed souls.

On Saturday — at six on the dot — we all thronged at Santa Rosa Park and began the procession to the house of Señora Sánchez. The parade stretched for blocks, winding all the way around El Paraiso Market where "El Chinito" Lee handed out

[3] afternoon dances
[4] shout (of enthusiasm, revelry)
[5] Saturday at seven o'clock at Mrs. Sánchez' house.

5

free saladitos[6] and lemonade, across the tracks and past the Sagrada Familia Church. Father Eliseo, who was just finishing confessions and not wanting to miss anything, joined the tail end of the gathering still wearing his chasuble.

And what a crowd! It was quite a sight to see: the compadres in their shiny jackets; the niños in their communion suits and dresses liberated from mothballed boxes for the occasion; the señoras somehow squeezed into their wedding dresses that had lain in cedar-lined chests through silver anniversaries; the teenaged girls in their quinceañera[7] duds kicking up the dust with stiletto heels; the vatos[8] perspiring in their starched collars and roper boots, six-packs dangling from their thumbs; the abuelitas in their flowered, ankle-length frocks embroidered with punta de cruz; the viudas, in black polyester, de luto como siempre;[9] the viejitos with their ancient guitars, leading the way.

Who would have thought that Señora Sánchez, thrice married and never one to attend daily mass or complete a novena or hold a vigil, would have witnessed a miracle? But strange are the ways of the Lord, y a cada santo le llega su día.[10] Even the Monseñor, skeptical, took time and stopped by to give his blessing, staying for a few minutes to visit, sitting stiffly on the faded velveteen sofa and drinking Nescafé from a cracked cup.

When the crowd arrived at the house of Señora Sánchez, the

---

[6] apricots soaked in brine and dried

[7] a Mexican custom in which 15-year-old girls are presented to society

[8] young men, "dudes"

[9] in mourning as always

[10] and every saint has his/her day

radio was blaring rancheras from the screenless kitchen window, Ave María. Señora Sánchez had made menudo and empanadas and teswín, and had strung multicolored lights out of season from the clothesline to the corners of the house to the roof of the rattletrap garage. Her numerous children were passing out the food and drink in paper bowls and cups on little metal trays. The dirt yard had been freshly watered to keep down the dust, and it smelled of earth after a rain. Tea roses, blooming unexpectedly in midsummer, clambered over the rickety trellises, across the rooftop, and into the trees, scenting the evening air like a chapel. Señora Sánchez' faithful cast-iron stove, propped up by a mesquite log at a corner where it was missing a leg, was festooned like an altar. It held all manner of flowers, fresh and paper and plastic, and votive candles and holy cards and rosaries and family photographs and religious medals and myriad ofrecimientos and tokens of her neighbors' reverence and good will.

And there we found Señora Guadalupe Sánchez, presiding in the middle of the freshly raked corral, the piocha blossoms fragrant at her feet. Her bare head was crowned by a halo from the street lamp, her lips moved silently with reverent gracias a Dioses, her mottled and veined hands were folded prayerfully over her ample belly — while everyone pushed and pressed to see . . .

the face of Christ . . .

in the tortilla.

Dichos

Proverbs

It's no fair. My Mamá sends me downtown every Saturday on the Old Pueblo bus line to visit my great-grandmother, Mamanina Agrippina. There is no arguing, neither, and that's that, no matter how much I act la chipeleada and pout.

All of my friends are off having a good time after chores, going to the early afternoon matinee at the Fox Theater — getting to stand in line and flirt with the boys, getting to see Roy Rogers and Dale Evans or a Zorro movie and the Mickey Mouse cartoon. But not me. Rain or shine, I'm on that bus and don't talk back neither.

No use pleading with my Papá. He mostly minds his own business and says that Mamá es la jefita. And he's always busy anyway, a cigarette dangling from his lips, his forehead furrowed in thought, fixing the leak on the roof or the leak under the sink or the leak under the hood of his car or the leak in the garden hose so he can water the street to keep the dust down.

So there it is. And here I am, sitting on my usual seat on the rickety bus, my legs sticking to the torn plastic seats, watching through the dust-streaked cracked windows for anything of interest so I don't die of boredom or have (as Sister Francisca warns me with her warm minty breath) impure thoughts.

And wouldn't you know it—the bus goes clanking down Congress Street just about the time the movie theater opens its doors for the twelve o'clock show. So I feel all worse, seeing my friends, Martita and Concha and Blanca, all dressed up fit to kill and wearing lipstick and face powder and eye shadow behind their mothers' backs. They're chewing gum and pushing and shoving in the line with the eighth-grade boys and acting so great.

I slouch down so they don't see me. It's just my luck, too—that cute guy Chuy Ramírez is there. He sits behind me in math and religion, and sometimes I think he likes me because he asks me to do his homework. But there he is, holding hands on the sly with la María Elena, who thinks she's so big because she has green eyes and wears a trainer bra. Blanca told me that he buys her a cherry coke and popcorn with real butter before the show. I haven't got a chance.

And me, in all my glory, what a square, with pigtails and saddle shoes and a hand-me-down dress that's a size too big, in the company of every old maid, widow, tía and abuelita from a hundred miles around. They've come to do their shopping at the Grand Central Market on Stone Avenue because Saturday is double-green-stamp day and the day los chinos bring in their fresh vegetables and flowers from their milpas[1] along the river.

The viejitas are dressed almost exactly the same: shapeless dark dresses down to their ankles; black priest shoes; thick cotton stockings; big old-fashioned earrings that make their lobes hang down; a huge gold medal with La Virgen de Guadalupe or El Sagrado Corazón; and all of them carrying enormous black leather purses that are bulging with Lord knows what. They look so ancient and frail that I can't figure out how they carry those heavy bolsas, but they do, and they spring off the bus without missing a step when it comes to a creaking stop in front of the Grand Central Market.

And me dragging my butt and feeling like a martyr. I have a list and some dollar bills that Mamá gave me crumpled up in my dress pocket. The list is always the same, more or less: a couple cans of Campbell soup of one kind or another (Mamanina told me once that she thought the Campbell Soup Kid looked like El Santo Niño, but she worried that he had las paperas y sarampión);[2] a package of manzanilla tea; fideo; frijoles; arroz; flour; lard; a couple chops of beef or pork; and cilantro, onion, chile, and tomato, unless they're in season in Mamanina's garden, which they usually are.

It's just a few blocks from the Grand Central Market to Barrio El Hoyo where my Mamanina lives. The house my Tatanino built, you couldn't miss it in a thousand years even if you

[1] cultivated fields

[2] the mumps and measles

try. For one thing, it's painted bright blue with yellow window-sills crowded with red and pink geraniums blooming in rusty Folgers coffee cans. And another thing, she trims all her front-yard hedges in the shapes of animals: a rooster, a peacock, a burro, a pig, a bull, a turkey, a cat, a dog. Never mind that they're all the same size. She says they remind her of her ran-chito in Jalisco, and they're a lot easier to take care of because she doesn't have to feed them or clean up after them.

If that's not enough, she has this big old shrine that my Tata-nino made her from river stones before he died. The nicho — well, it looks like a crowded bus stop if you ask me, with all those statues and pictures of every virgin and saint and every Santo Niño of this or that under the sun. Some I'll bet you've never ever heard of, like Los Santos Cuates, who if you pray to them, they keep visitors away; or San Expedito, who keeps them from staying too long; or San Lázaro, who will burn your house or car up if you don't keep your manda; or San Antonio, who helps you find things — sometimes even a husband or boy-friend. All the good he has done me.

My Mamanina has the shrine all decorated with plastic ferns and flowers from El Kresge's, and fresh flowers, too, and some from last year's velación[3] that are all dried up; and pretty peb-bles and driftwood from the Santa Cruz River; and seashells and starfish that relatives brought her from California; and Christmas bells and balls and tinsel garlands; and a candle that is always burning; and two or three strings of multicolored,

---

[3] vigil or prayers to a saint

blinking Christmas lights that she keeps lit all year round be-cause, she says, "Every day should be like Christmas."

You won't believe it, neither, when I tell you that I'll bet every single flower growing in my Mamanina's garden around that nicho is named after Saint Somebody-or-Other, like the Barritas de San José or San Miguelito or Lirios del Sagrado Corazón or Lágrimas de María or Cornetas del Angel Gabriel or Rosas Guadalupanas or Trompillos del Angel de la Guardia or Flor de Santa Catarina.

I tell you, I get in a better mood the minute I turn the corner and see that shrine.

She's waiting for me, so brown and small, in the doorway under the porch like she knows the exact time I'm going to arrive. She's wearing this big old apron with gigantic pockets that's made out of old flour sacks — "La Piña" it says today, and on other days it's "La Azteca" or "La Rosa." She's so glad to see me, like always, and she gives me this big old hug and pulls a treat for me, a saladito, out of one of the pockets. Sometimes it's a pan dulce or membrillo or a piece of gum. I never know what's going to come out of those pockets.

I help her put away the groceries in the kitchen. It smells so good because she's always cooking something on her wood-burning stove. I settle into the little chair she keeps for me by the big black stove, and I watch her while she pours flour into a mound in a big clay bowl so she can make tortillas. She adds the baking powder and the salt in the form of a cross, "to bless the bread," she says solemnly. I watch while she rolls the tortillas out perfect and round like a Communion host, and she gives me one right off the comal, all warm and bubbly with melting butter. I am waiting hungrily for the guiso in the simmering pot to be done.

I have to talk to her in Spanish because she never learned any English, only a few words like "enough is too many." Besides, she says, "What for? No one in this old barrio speaks English anyway, and I'm going back to my ranchito in Mexico someday." Sometimes I can't think of a word, or I pronounce something funny or use the wrong verb, and she corrects me but never criticizes.

"Oh, Mamanina," I sigh, "esta tortilla está tan sabrosa."[4]

She smiles. "Cuando hay hambre, no hay mal pan,"[5] she says all humble-like. And all the time she's pat-pat-patting and rolling out tortillas, she's keeping her eye on the simmering pot and stirring with a big wooden spoon or adding a pinch of this or that.

I am taking big bites out of the tortilla and gulping it down, and the butter is running down my arm, but she doesn't scold.

"To tell you the truth, Mamanina," I confide in my halting Spanish, "I didn't have a very good week."

"De la olla a la boca a todos se le cae la sopa,"[6] she consoles.

"Sister Francisca, she picks on me. She said I was passing notes and talking in history class, and she scolded me, and I didn't do nothing, I swear. The trouble is, I talked back and

---

[4] This tortilla is delicious.

[5] When one is hungry, there's no bad bread.

[6] Everyone spills a little bit of soup. (No one is perfect.)

said, 'It's no fair. I didn't do it,' so I got double time in detention and a note sent home to Mamá and Papá."

"En boca cerrada no entra mosca,"[7] she chides gently.

"It's that María Elena," I say enviously. "She thinks she's so great. She's a teacher's pet, and she shows off and wears a new outfit to school every week."

"No jusgues el hombre por su vestido; Dios hizo el uno, el sastre el otro,"[8] she opines soothingly as she spoons out steaming ladles of the guiso into two clay bowls.

"My friends, they're lucky. They get to go to the movies every week and sometimes to the roller-skating rink."

"Luz de la calle, obscuridad de la casa,"[9] she warns.

"And they never invite me," I whine.

"Al nopal van a ver nomás cuando tiene tunas,"[10] she comforts.

We are sitting at her small kitchen table now under the brown limpid gaze of the apostles at the Last Supper. I am tearing off pieces of tortillas and making little scoops to eat the guiso with. Mamá doesn't let me do that at home; she says it is muy ranchero to sopear.

"Anyway, Mamanina," I announce, to soften my litany of complaints, "next year when I'm in the ninth grade and in high

---

[7] Flies don't fly into a closed mouth. (Silence is golden.)

[8] Don't judge a man by his clothes; God made one, a tailor made the other. (Clothes don't make the man.)

[9] Light in the street, darkness in the house. (Charity begins at home.)

[10] They only go visit the prickly pear when it has fruit. (They are fair-weather friends.)

school I'm going to try harder, and it will all be better, you'll see."

"Poco a poco se anda lejos,"[11] she answers encouragingly as she wipes one of my spills on the red-and-white oilcloth with her napkin.

The afternoon wears on. I help with the dishes, the sweeping and the dusting, the changing of the bed, and the washing in that old wringer washer out on the back porch. I hang the clothes out on the clothesline to dry because the day is sunny. Before I know it, it's time for me to hurry so I can catch the last cross-town bus.

I give her a hug as I say goodbye, "Hasta la semana que entra."[12] I run out of the house, slamming the screen door in my haste.

I'm running down the street, and I turn to look back before I turn the corner. I see her with her hand lifted up in a blessing. She's so small, so small, framed in her doorway like one of those faded little old saints in her shrine.

My panza is full of that blessed bread.

The breeze is in my face. I have wings on my feet and angels at my back.

No se puede repicar y en la procesión andar.[13]

---

[11] Little by little one goes a long way.

[12] Until next week.

[13] You can't ring the bell and be in the procession too. (You can't be in two places at once.)

La Toreadora

The Bullfighter

It happened like clockwork, the first Sunday of every month after the noon mass when the echo of the final bells of Santa Margarita Church unraveled in skeins of sound into the vast blue sky.

(The bellringer was the ancient Spanish priest, Padre Bartolomé, an octogenarian, who wheezed as he pulled the heavy bell ropes, having suffered from asthma all these years in the dust of this godforsaken desert frontier so far from the verdant olive groves of his beloved Andalucía. He still spoke with the Castilian lisp, and even after six decades of service in Barrio Hollywood, he had never learned to sopear with tortillas or eat nopalitos or menudo. He still clung stubbornly to his continental custom of a midnight supper of eggs fried in olive oil, crusty bread, and vino tinto. His only consolation — for now he was too decrepit to return to his homeland — was that the

Almighty would grant him a very high place in heaven far away from his earthly charges, where he could spend an eternity in the green expanses of a paradise that resembled southern Spain, in the erudite company of other gachupines.[1])

Right on time, the buquis[2] started drifting in to abuelita's ("Grande" we called her) corral, peering through the spiny curtain of nopales[3] or the spiked fence of carrizo before inching their barefooted, dusty way in to their favorite vantage points for watching the spectacle. The arena was a circle defined by the chicken coop, the cottonwood tree, the garden, a scraggly tamarisk, a lean-to ramada that held all manner of automobile parts, rickety chairs, and a magnificent cast-iron wood-burning stove (only mesquite leña would do) where Grande worked her magic, cooking her paper-thin tortillas sonorenses that were as transparent as organdy and as big as the moon.

A montón de chavalos[4] — the regulars — arrived next. First came Los Cuates, so identical that we called them "Primero" and "Segundo" interchangeably. No matter, they both answered to the same name. They picked a shady spot next to the cottonwood tree and sat like silhouetted bookends, their skinny legs drawn up, their curly brown heads resting on their knees in polite anticipation. "Ay, qué bien educados," our

[1] Spaniards born in Spain
[2] kids; brats
[3] prickly-pear cactus
[4] bunch of kids

mother sighed, holding them up as examples of comportment in contrast to our tomboy ways.

"El Chango" Morales arrived and scurried lithely up the rough gray bark of the old cottonwood to hang upside down from the tallest branch so he could view the proceedings in reverse. (Our mother was always concerned that all the blood rushing to El Chango's brain might affect him adversely, but the opposite proved to be true. He excelled in academics and later went on to become president of a small junior college in eastern Arizona. When he returned home on vacations, he was the subject of much good-natured ribbing about whether his success was attributable to his simian quickness and agility or the extra oxygen to his gray matter.)

"La Reina" Esparza made her entrance with great flourish, wearing a tilting crown of aluminum foil and her Communion dress and veil, now tattered and yellowed after three summers of punishment. She had outgrown it by now, of course; the seams were bursting and the torn lace ruffle was trailing in the dirt. She took her place with much aplomb, seating herself in her wooden wagon among the scruffy dolls that were her ladies-in-waiting. My sister and I consistently and vociferously refused to be members of her royal court. She did not disappoint her ambitious and long-suffering mother—years later she would charm her way into the hearts of the Chamber of Commerce members and become the first mexicana Rodeo Queen for the century-old La Fiesta de los Vaqueros.

Next to arrive was "La Minnie" Gonzales, so called because she wore two black ponytails drawn up in ovals on the sides of her head, and her high-pitched voice resembled the squeak of her tocaya,[5] the famous Disney mouse. She was the only one who wore shoes (black patent Mary Janes) after church, and my sister and I were green with envy. She sat herself carefully down on one of the rickety chairs in the ramada, having been cautioned by her mother, who prided herself on her daughter's fair complexion, to stay out of the sun.

Louie, "The Foot," was the last to arrive, leaving his huge footprints in the dust, the shirttails of his oversized hand-me-down shirts fluttering. He would sit as close to La Reina as possible, but she paid him no mind, turning her regal head away from him and sniffing decorously upwind. (He would have the last laugh, however, growing up to be the handsomest vato from the barrio with the easiest smile and winningest ways. While pumping gas on the freeway, he was recruited by a Hollywood scout to play the Indian sidekick to a gavacho[6] cowboy on a TV western. And now his oversized feet trip the light fantastic in $500 snakeskin boots with sterling silver tips while La Reina eats her heart out working as a checkout girl in the Southgate Shopping Center.)

With perfect timing, like a matador when the bullring is packed and restless, Grande marched out into the yard, the kitchen screen door slamming behind her. The white strands of hair from her molote had come undone with her urgency, her flour-sack apron was tied primly at her waist, and the tongues

[5] namesake
[6] Anglo

of her laceless high-top tennies (her "chicken-killing shoes") flapped with each stride.

As if on cue from a baton-wielding conductor, a cacophony of sound arose from the direction of the gallinero. The residents of the coop squawked hysterically in the eternal wisdom of chickens who smell death in the air.

Grande strode into the pen and with her expert's eye chose the fattest, most succulent fowl (and not incidentally, the laziest layer) from the feathered pandemonium. She planted herself firmly in the middle of the circle of onlookers and admirers, hugging the protesting chicken while small white feathers drifted to the ground like snow.

The bola of us kids strained our bodies forward in rapt attention, our chattering hushed to reverent silence. It was over almost as soon as it began: a swift and expert twist, the severed head thrown to the waiting alley cat, the flopping body running erratically, spurting blood from its headless neck. All of us buquis screeched and scrambled to get out of the way of the hapless, careening animal.

Grande then mercifully placed a No. 2 tina[7] over the dying gallina (whose body had not received the tragic news from its diminutive, detached brain that it was dead), and in its mortal throes, it beat its tinny dance of death against the sides of the metal tub.

The sacrifice was complete. And oh! What a worthy and noble death was celebrated and commemorated later that eve-

[7] tub

ning in ambrosial platters and pots of gallina con mole, or perhaps gallina con pipian, or arroz con pollo, or pollo frito, or caldo de pollo, the steam and aromas rising from Grande's stove like incense from an ancient altar!

But first Grande paraded not once, not twice, but three times around the inside of the circle of admiring children, twirling her red cape, prancing in small steps in her tiny brocade slippers, doffing her velvet, three-cornered hat. Her suit of lights caught the rays of the midafternoon sun and blinded us as she promenaded to the fanfare of trumpets and drums.

And we threw her red and white roses of love and courage and victory, as we cheered and cheered and cheered. ¡Olé! ¡Olé! ¡Olé!

Bordados

Embroidery

Our mother, being proper, always worried about que iba pensar la gente,[1] so we wore our homemade, floral-print dresses long-sleeved, with piqué Peter Pan collars, and twelve inches off the floor. She measured our hems with scientific accuracy using her yellow yardstick, circa 1950, from Mulcahey Lumber, while we rotated slowly in our stockinged feet on the coffee table.

Summer slumber parties or tap dance lessons, forget it. No swimming in public pools either, or coed picnic outings to Sabino Canyon with the choir, or roller-skating in short skirts (twirl, twirl) con las americanas. Instead, we had rosary every evening, confession every Saturday, and communion every Sunday, under her watchful eye.

In the endless summer afternoons, after chores of dusting, sweeping, mopping, polishing, washing, hanging, starching,

[1] what people would think

and ironing, she kept our hands and our hearts busy embroidering our trousseaus in brilliant silken threads — "De Colores."[2] Hand towels and kitchen towels, pillowcases and dresser scarves, handkerchiefs and aprons, dreams and desires, piled up neatly in cedar-scented chests.

I was obedient and a perfectionist, and became an expert at the French knot, the daisy chain, and the cross-stitch — hemming in my passions with tiny even stitches — only rarely straying from the dime-store patterns of flowers, vines, birds, and maidens all in a row.

But at times, with trembling hand and sweating upper lip, I would prick myself with her golden needle while wondering what in the world it felt like to be kissed.

[2] song that celebrates the colors of life

Paraíso

Paradise

The police had been having trouble that year with the winos littering the park with their disheveled presence. They frightened me as I walked home from Immaculate Heart Convent School, deliberately scuffing my brown leather oxfords, my beige regulation uniform stained with lunch and dusted with chalk. My knees would still be smarting from the hour spent on the hard wooden kneeler in front of the chapel altar as penance for my impertinence during catechism class. ("But why can't girls be priests?" "How can Mary be a virgin if she's a mother?")

Sister Consuelo's thin scolding would still be ringing in my ears ("wastes time, is inattentive, annoys others"). My math and spelling papers, rolled up in my sweaty schoolgirl hands, were webbed with her spidery red script ("incomplete, careless work").

My mother always warned me to walk home the other way and to stand up straight and pick up my feet when I walked.

But there was something about those unshaven men and their rumpled companionship that drew me at a careful distance — groups of them lounging greenly in their stained clothes under the trees at Armory Park, breathing in the sun-dappled air or sleeping off the soup-kitchen tuna surprise and the cheap Tokay, playing greasy pinochle under the shadows of birds in flight and song, their past sorrows and their future dreams blurred by unconsecrated wine.

Orgullo

Pride

Our great-aunt Doña Petra de Alba Cárdenas Ortiz López del Castillo de la Torre had gone into seclusion. She was receiving no callers, except the Bishop. This somber announcement by our mother sent my sister and me ("las dos diablitas," to quote our great-aunt) into paroxysms of hidden glee and feigned disappointment.

How we dreaded our required Sunday afternoon visits, admonished to behave by our proper mother every mile of the trip across town to Tía Petra's house! Act like señoritas. Sit quietly. Speak when spoken to. Walk, don't run. These cautionary reminders were replaced by mild reprimands on the return trip home. Somehow, we always failed to live up to our gentle mother's expectations.

Our Great-Aunt Doña Petra de Alba Cárdenas Ortiz López del Castillo de la Torre had the finest house on the block on the old

Camino Real in the historic, downtown Old Pueblo. In fact, she had the only house on the block, the other venerable dwellings of the colonial period having fallen prey to the higher necessities of a community center and parking lot. It was no accident that our family's sturdy Sonoran manse had been saved from the wrecker's ball: the Pioneer Historical and Preservation Auxiliary had determined that William Sutton, a nineteenth-century territorial governor — and as scurrilous an adventurer, scalawag, and fortune seeker as any to kick up dust in the Pimería Alta — had dined there one night in the trusting company of high Spanish society. This had not been documented or verified, but it was enough to commute the sentence that had befallen the other eighteenth-century adobe haciendas of the vecindad.

The city fathers had become owners of the house as a result of condemnation proceedings, but our great-aunt was allowed the right of survivorship until her death. (After her demise, the house would become a territorial museum and gift shop, with a bronze plaque on the corner attesting to its historical significance.)

But during our childhood Tía Petra held court there every Sunday afternoon to a steady stream of relatives who crossed the rickety threshold into the zaguán[1] and faithfully paid her their respects. She was proud, no doubt about it. She was the dowager matriarch of a large and extended family — unto the third

---

[1] a very wide doorway or entrance popular in traditional Mexican architecture

cousins — over whom she held unexplainable sway. The ter-
tulias[2] were a requirement; we'd be hauled there after mass
by our dutiful mother, Tía Petra's favorite niece and the only
child of her youngest sister. We were sentenced to sit stiffly
on straight-backed chairs in the dim parlor under the stern gaze
of our ancestors' portraits, our black-patent Mary Janes dangling, the lacy collars and anklets of our Sunday best itching.

We sipped lemonade and ate biscochitos while the adults
conversed, our mother's final admonishment ringing in our
ears: "Pórtense bien,[3] or else!" So, nos portamos bien as best we
could, knowing that any serious transgressions would be paid
for later, or sooner as the case might be: our great-aunt, never
being one to spare anything, much less the rod, was not reluc-
tant to tap us gingerly on the head with her silver-handled
walking stick if she noticed the slightest breach of propriety on
our part.

The only thing of interest to my sister and me during those
endless tedious afternoons was the pampered, white Persian cat
who sat regally on our great-aunt's bony lap and glared disdain-
fully at us through slitted yellow eyes while Tía petted her with
slender, beringed hands. Another distraction was the resplendent garden in the patio that was lush with citrus trees, a two-
hundred-year-old fig, and a tangle of vines and flowers. The
pièce de résistance in the arbor was an old stone well. For

---

[2] a Mexican custom of gathering with family and friends on Sunday afternoons for
conversation, music, and refreshments

[3] You'd better behave.

unknown reasons Tía Petra had preserved it, complete with the antique chain, lever, and bucket that in the past century had serviced the needs of the once ample household, descendants of our great-grandfather to the power of the fifth, the gachupín,[4] Don Estanislao de la Torre. The prospects for the haughty feline presented by the bucket and the well — when the cover was lifted, the well still shone damply and smelled greenly from its mysterious depths — entertained us. We endured our boredom by plotting in whispers the mayhem we might inflict once adult attention was diverted for sufficient time to the aforementioned gato creido.

Other than that, our precious childhood hours ticked away in cadence with the old brass clock on the mantel while we watched through the transparent lace-curtained windows for any street activity that might distract us — stray dogs, cart-pushing vendors, lucky urchins in glorious freedom playing kick-the-can. The adult conversation — always the same theme but with a continually changing cast of characters — droned on in the background. The afternoon sun slanted its dusty beams lower and lower in the gloomy sala crowded with Victorian bric-a-brac and a jumble of overstuffed Edwardian furniture that swooped and curved, culminating in arm rests and feet carved with the likenesses of beasts and birds of prey.

It was in such a seat that Great-Aunt Doña Petra de Alba Cárdenas Ortiz López del Castillo de la Torre held court. She sat on a high-backed settee with lion's feet and a backrest that

[4] Spaniard born in Spain

was carved with the de la Torre coat of arms—a crenelated tower with an eagle and a sable wolf on a blue background of stars with the word "Pureza" encircling the design. It was from this direction that most of the one-sided conversation emanated, with our mother or other hapless relatives in attendance nodding solemnly in agreement or exclaiming, "¡No me digas![5] . . . ¡Jesús, María y José! . . . ¡Gracias a Dios! . . . ¡No lo creo! .[6] . . !Tiene Ud. razón!"[7] or interrupting Tía just long enough to ask her if she wanted more café con leche.

"I have received word," Tía announced one Sunday in her grandiloquent way, "that your second cousin thrice removed, Beatriz Urrea, has married well: Juan Martínez, a Californiano from the Suástegui family of the Santa Barbara Hacienda. His great-great-great grandfather was the governor of Baja California, and he is connected through his mother's sister's husband's great-uncle to the Figueroa family of the San Rafael land grant." She paused to take a wheezing breath, waved her white hand at nothing, and droned on: "Qué lástima about Rafaelita Figueroa, the patrona of the San Rafael, who was descended from Hermengildo Salcido, who came from Sevilla and served under the great conquistador Francisco Coronado. 'Tis said she never married because she could not find anyone in those wilds that was equal to her lineage and station. That is why the family holdings went to her New Mexico cousins, the Montoyas

---

[5] You don't say!

[6] I don't believe it!

[7] You have your reasons!

(to whom, I need not remind you, we are related through our great-grandmother Consuelo's husband's sister-in-law), who are connected through marriage to the explorer and comandante of the Tucson presidio, Capitán Guillermo Velarde de la Madrid. His wife was a niece of Carlota, and she served as a lady-in-waiting in the French court of Maximilian. Ah, those were the days, when breeding and elegance and dignity prevailed! Now where was I? Oh yes, your prima, Beatriz." She sniffed delicately into her monogrammed handkerchief. "Well, if I do say so, her brother Narciso did not fare so well. It is said he is betrothed to a young woman from the Romero mercantile family." She whispered now, "I understand they ran mule teams, of all things, over the Sierras to the port at Guaymas and back again with ship cargoes to Alamos before the days of that awful revolution. ¡Arrieros! They claim connection to the Almadas of the Fuerte Silver Mines, but really, whom do they think they are kidding? Once a muleteer, always a muleteer, if you ask me. Money isn't everything. It's blood that counts, and they don't even have their own pew at the cathedral!

"At least I have been spared that great pena. Thanks to our social standing and my discreet efforts, my only daughter, Catalina, as you all know, is married to a Roybal from Santa Fe with a pedigree three feet long. Puros españoles."

She was breathless now, pausing to finger the heirloom filigree cross that rested on her throat as if to bless herself, her words, and her progeny. Then she pronounced haughtily, "Bueno, como dice el dicho: 'Aunque la mona se vista de seda,

32

mona se queda.' "[8] She snapped shut her white-lace fan, signaling the end of the tertulia.

Well, yes, la Doña Petrita had gone into seclusion. She was receiving no callers, except the Bishop. She had taken to sighing and wearing her widow's weeds even to bed, praying through the night on her antique ivory beads, hardly taking time to eat, and then only Holy Communion and chicken broth. She was descended from conquistadores, sangre pura, green-eyed blancos y cristianos who had fallen on hard times, but they still had their pride and their good name and their breeding, gracias a Dios for that.

Pero en mejor paño cae la mancha,[9] and Doña Petrita was inconsolable, not understanding how Tata Dios meted out his justice on descendientes, not accepting that against all odds, her first grandchild had been born moreno, with curly black hair, high cheekbones, and black almond-shaped eyes.

Bueno, como dice el dicho: El que se viste de ajeno, en la calle lo desnudan.[10]

---

[8] Well, as the proverb says: "A monkey dressed in silk is still a monkey." (Clothes don't make the man.)

[9] Even the best handkerchief can get stained. (No one is perfect.)

[10] The person who dresses in someone else's clothes may find himself naked in the street. (Pride goeth before a fall.)

La Bendición

The Blessing

So far so good.

Nana Tacha is busy patrolling her garden with the dedication of a decorated foot soldier on watch, padding between the rows of chilies and tomatoes in her chanclas — flip-flop — pinching off the aphids with her bare fingers, stopping to pull a bothersome weed, scolding the birds, shooing the chickens, gathering ripened figs in a chipped blue enameled pan, snipping pieces of hierba buena for today's soups or stews.

I'm in the back bedroom keeping an eye on Nana Tacha through a lace-curtained window, hoping she will remain distracted and otherwise occupied so my sister and I can make our escape without her noticing. I can see the white molote of her silken hair floating as if disembodied, like a wispy summer cloud, behind the stand of hollyhocks beside the bedroom window.

If all goes as planned, she will march on to the shady east

side of the house to inspect her rose garden, which she will then water tenderly with a leaky garden hose. ("Tenemos que tener rosas para la Virgen,"[1] she says.) The noon Angelus bell will ring, and she will pause to sing a few alabanzas in front of the grotto of La Virgen de Guadalupe that is located in the middle of the fragrant arbor. She will then collect dried rose petals and rose hips in the pocket of her apron for fever teas and perfumed baths in the doldrums of summer.

From there she'll go on to check on her spring annuals — carnations, geraniums, petunias, larkspur, sweet peas, and irises — flowering in a cleared space beside the backyard ramada. The flowers are blooming at attention in every imaginable container left over from our grandfather's household and automobile repairs — a cracked claw-footed tub, a toilet without a seat, discarded wheel rims, tires punctured beyond repair, a rusty sink, an old wringer washer that is listing like a distressed ship on its corroded legs.

"Mi jardín es muy artístico," Nana Tacha says with pride.

If our luck holds, the garden is good for another fifteen minutes. . . .

I'm racing around the bedroom packing our paraphernalia for the citywide CYO picnic and swim party. There's baby oil, combs, brushes, towels, cover-ups and hats (our mother insisted), those hated bathing suits with three inches of modest ruffles at the bodice and at the thigh, and a stack of paperback

---

[1] We must have roses for the Virgin.

books gathered conspicuously in our parents' presence to gain their good will for future excursions.

I'm trying to decide which potions, creams, lotions, unguents, colognes, and hairsprays to choose from among the clutter on our vanity. Presiding over the debris on the dressing table is a statue of St. Teresa the Little Flower — given to my sister and me by our ever-optimistic mother that we might meditate on the example of her exemplary life. The ceramic likeness of the teenaged Carmelite nun, dressed modestly in a brown-and-white religious habit with a spray of pink roses in her arms, gazes glassily and piously on my disheveled room and frenetic activities. She has a perfect figure and features, with ivory skin and rosy cheeks. She decided when she was an adolescent that she wanted to go to the convent and be the bride of Christ. Give me a break!

My sister is clattering around in the kitchen packing our lunch in paper bags — bologna sandwiches, lemonade, potato chips, store-bought cookies, and apples. She has deftly hidden at the back of the icebox the burros and empanadas that Nana Tacha made for us. I hear the sound of slamming cupboard doors and then the tinkling noise of shattering glass followed by a mild expletive: "Chi . . . huahua!"

It's a few minutes till countdown. We're tearing around making sure that we've thought of everything and keeping our ears alert for the beep-beep-de-beep announcing the arrival of our ride.

It is the first time that we have been given permission to go on such an outing and the first time we have been allowed to ride in a car with our friends unchaperoned by a parent. ("But Mamá and Papá, we're in high school already!")

Riding in cars with boys unaccompanied by an adult is an occasion of sin according to chapter two, page 45, of our religious studies manual. It is a favorite topic of our stern and ever-vigilant pastor, Father Estanislao.

The driver of the car and trusted chauffeur is our best friend Graciela's older brother, Luis Carlos. He is a senior, a little stout, wears glasses, and is considered unattractive. It is rumored that he is going to the seminary in the fall. Our parents, it goes without saying, approve. They pride themselves on their unerring ability to judge a person's character at a glance.

(They proved wrong about Luis Carlos. He eloped with a carhop from the Double LL drive-in during the second summer vacation from his priestly studies. He started out doing yard-work to support his bride and is now the president of a citywide landscaping business, which is most fortunate, because it now employs in some capacity or other every one of their large brood of eight children. His mother, Doña Amparo, never has recovered from the disgrace and disappointment and is still making yearly pilgrimages on her knees to San Francisco in Magdalena in the hope that her favorite son will resume his vocation.)

Beep-beep-de-beep!

"They're here," we shout simultaneously to one another as we tear around the house gathering up our various bags and bundles. Our heads are pounding with excitement.

38

Nana Tacha suddenly materializes in the back doorway of the kitchen like a genie from a bottle.

We give each other a dismayed glance. Our hearts sink. Oh no, she will want to give us her blessing, and we'll be late for sure.

"You cannot leave until you receive la bendición," she announces sweetly but firmly in her lilting Spanish. She points to a spot on the living room floor. "Come and kneel here."

Beep-beep-de-beep!

There is no escape, so we do as we are told. We kneel on the hooked rug covering the flower-patterned linoleum. She raises her open hand and holds it over our heads in much the same manner as the Pope blessing the throngs from his balcony at the Vatican.

She begins by invoking the entire hosts of heaven· "Que La Virgen de Guadalupe y La Virgen de San Juan de Los Lagos y La Virgen del Perpetuo Socorro y La Virgen del Rosario y La Virgen del Carmen y La Inmaculada Concepción . . ."

Beep-beep-de-beep!

I glance nervously out the living room window. The car motor is idling, and Luis Carlos is drumming his fingers impatiently on the steering wheel.

Nana Tacha is unfazed. She doesn't miss a beat.

". . . y El Santo Niño de Atocha y El Santo Niño de Praga y Los Dulces Nombres y La Sagrada Familia y San José y San Antonio y San Judas y San Miguel y San Martín de Porres y San Francisco y San Isidro y San Cristóbal . . ."

Beep-beep-de-beep-de-beep-de-beep!

I start to squirm. My sister lets me have it in the ribs with her sharp elbow.

". . . y La Santa Trinidad y La Mano Poderoso de Dios y El Sagrado Corazón y El Cristo Crucificado y Resuscitado (here she genuflects and makes the sign of the cross) las guie y las proteja de socialistas, comunistas, Villistas, Carrancistas, Maderistas, huelguistas, federales . . ."[2]

I'm thinking about my knees pressing into the ridged and bumpy throw. Oh great! Now they're going to look all creased and puckered.

". . . protestantes, Jehovas, mormones, Aleluyas, ateistas, bandidos, ladrones, mentirosos, embusteros, asesinatos, mafiosos, drogeros, pachucos . . ."[3]

Drops of nervous perspiration are beginning to roll down the insides of my arms.

Nana Tacha continues in her sing-song Tapatío voice, "y que no tengan accidente y que no se choquen y que no se envenenen y que no se pierdan y que no las piquen víboras ni abejas y que lleguen a la casa buenas y sanas y santas. Amen."[4]

"Amen," we echo solemnly, feigning piety.

We give her a peck on the cheek, grab our belongings, and

---

[2] . . . guide and protect you from socialists, communists, followers of Villa, Carranza, or Madera, striking laborers, federalists . . .

[3] . . . Protestants and other religious groups that aren't Catholic, atheists, bandits, thieves, liars, fakers, assassins, Mafia, drug users and pushers . . .

[4] and that you don't have an accident or have a wreck or be poisoned or get lost or be stung by snakes or bees, and that you return to the house whole, healthy, and holy.

bolt out the front door. We're just in time. Luis Carlos has already put the car in gear.

"Guy!" Graciela scolds. "What took you so long? We told you to be ready on the dot. We almost left without you. Now we're gonna be late."

"Oh, it was nothing," we lie with relief as we scramble into the back seat of the wood-paneled station wagon. "Our Nana Tacha just wanted to say goodbye." We smile secretly to each other as the car pulls away.

¡Cuiden sus gallinas que los gallos andan sueltos![5]

---

[5] Take care of your chickens for the roosters are loose!

Reinas

Queens

I don't know what Mamá was thinking of when she named me Reina and my sister Czarina. The only way she got away with it was because she tacked on the names María Ana and María Elena in the middle to appease our grandmother. You have to have a saint's name at baptism and confirmation, or it doesn't count. Those are the rules, and our abuelita knows them better than the Bishop. I guess I shouldn't be complaining. If Nana had had her way, we would have been named after the saint's day on which we were born. Then we would have had to suffer through Gertrudis and Clotilde.

My sister, Czarina María Elena, is twenty-three years old now, and I am a year younger. She looks the czarina part, tall and slim and beautiful like Mamá, with wavy black hair and an aristocratic nose. Me? No matter how hard I try or how much I practice and fuss in front of the mirror, I still can't look the part.

Everybody except Mamá still calls me "Chapa."[1] I hate that name.

But Mamá is blinded by love, and she thinks we're both beautiful princesses — except my sister is the swan, and I am the duckling. Mamá dressed us like twins until we were thirteen years old and in junior high. Then my sister put up a big fuss and locked herself in our bedroom, refusing to come out or eat until Mamá agreed to let her pick out her own clothes and her own Simplicity and Butterick dress patterns without me having a carbon copy. That was fine with me because I was too much of a tomboy for all those frills anyhow.

Mamá keeps an album of our baby and childhood photos handy on the coffee table, and she shows them to anyone who can't make it out the door fast enough. I swear she'd have a glass case built just to display some of those gowns and dresses she sewed for us — like they have for the wives of the presidents of the United States in the Smithsonian in Washington, D.C. I saw a special about it on TV.

The whole queen thing started with our baptismal gowns. They were cotton batiste with rows and rows of pintucks and lace that Mamá sewed on by hand, with little pink roses em-broidered around the neck and sleeves and hem, hats with satin trim and pink ribbons, and satin slips too. For heaven's sake, who needs a slip when you're only six months old!

Mamá has our eight-by-ten baptismal photographs on the living room wall. We're wearing tiny gold earrings and brace-

[1] "Shorty"

44

lets and little shoes that she crocheted herself. She had the shoes bronzed, and they're sitting on the phonograph as bookends holding up our baby scrapbooks. How embarrassing.

She saved those baptismal gowns. They're in a box with cedar chips under her and Papá's bed — just in case she had another girl, I guess, which she never did. I don't know what she would have named her — probably Duquesa María or Marquesa María something.

Our First Communion was an even bigger production. Our dresses were organdy batiste, long, with little trains and three tiers in the skirts, and capped sleeves that came to a point at the wrists, and scalloped necklines decorated with tiny seed pearls.

Mamá sewed them on her treadle sewing machine, the one that she inherited from her mother, our other grandmother, Mercedes. It had the name Singer embossed on it in gold, and red and blue flowers painted on the arm, and all the little drawers were carved with roses and lilies and vines.

I remember the light burning late at night in the corner of our big kitchen where Mamá kept that old Singer. Clackety, clack, whir, whir. She'd sew after she'd done the dishes and a load of wash and ironed a basketful and swept and read to us and tucked us into bed and fed our baby brother and put him to bed too. (He had a real name, Alfredo Anselmo, but his nickname was "El Rey.")

Clackety, clack, whir, whir. The yards and yards of snowy white fabric and lace flowed between her deft, slender fingers, pooling like snowbanks onto a sheet on the kitchen floor. Her elegant head was bent over in the dim light, her face deter-

45

mined and furrowed in concentration, the thick locks of her mestiza hair falling into her eyes.

She even bought us little rhinestone crowns to wear with our Communion veils. Sister Theodosia discouraged it, but Mamá was undaunted. She had to order them special from Saccani's in Nogales to get them small enough. Even after all that trouble, mine didn't fit and kept tilting during mass until the little crown finally obeyed the law of gravity and clattered to the floor during the recessional, only to be scooped up by that smirking altar boy José. He thought he was so great because his mother was the president of the Guadalupanas. He never let me forget it either, calling me "Corona Pedona"[2] under his breath every time he passed me in the hallway at school.

When we were sophomores in high school we had to be Florecita debutantes—because Mamá said so—at the League of Mexican American Women's 16 de Septiembre Fiesta en Xochimilco Quinceañera Ball at the Tucson Community Center Grand Ballroom. There was no way I could get out of it. Mamá didn't pay her dues and go to all those meetings all those years for nothing.

Mamá must have saved her pennies a long time for that extravaganza because it wasn't cheap, and she had Florecitas two years in a row. My sister was first because she was fifteen in August, and I followed the next July.

The dresses were picked by a committee of the League ladies. They were the most elaborate dresses I've ever seen, with big

[2] "Stinky Queen" (literally, "flatulant, stinky crown")

puffed sleeves (if a strong wind had come up, I'd have been airborne), a shirred bodice that looked ridiculous on me because I had no boobs, and a narrow velvet belt that would have looked great if I'd had a waist. I felt like a cow in that dress!

We had to practice for the ball for hours and hours after school at the home of the League president. We curtsied and bowed and pirouetted and walked with books on our heads so when we came down the spiral staircase at the ballroom we would be graceful and not stumble and fall. To top it off, on Saturday mornings we had to go for instruction at the convent, and Sister Eloisa told us all about the history of the quinceañera.[3] She said it went back a million years to the Aztecs, our ancestors, who had a ceremony when young girls came of age. She went on and on about purity and modesty and generosity and humility and obedience and how they would help us to be good daughters and sisters and wives and mothers. She said we should model our lives after the saints, especially the Virgin Mary, Mother of God, Queen of the Heavens, Patron of the Americas, and Empress of the Universe.

The big night finally arrived, and everyone was excited. All our relatives came to the ball, and I managed to make it down the staircase without falling. I had to do a minuet with my Papá (something old-fashioned that dated back to the French court of Maximilian and Carlota at Chapultepec). He was so handsome in his rented tuxedo, a red carnation pinned in his lapel, his face all sweaty from nervousness, his eyes gleaming and

[3] a Mexican custom in which 15-year-old girls are presented to society (debutantes)

proud as I tripped over his newly shined shoes doing five-eighths time to the two-quarter music while the orchestra of Louie León played.

I could see Mamá out of the corner of my eyes, looking so regal, beaming from a ringside table decorated with Mexican paper flowers and the Mexican flag and little gondolas like the ones in the real Xochimilco. She looked like a queen. Her luxuriant hair was drawn back in a chignon held together with a rhinestone clip. She was wearing a cocktail dress of blue peau de soie that she had made herself; it was the same color as the bottle of Midnight in Paris perfume that she had on the little glass tray on her dresser.

My sister Czarina María Elena was standing beside her, smiling smugly because she had done the routine perfectly last year and had been voted Miss Talent and Miss Congeniality. Her escort had been Xavier Gallegos, the most popular guy at school, president of the senior class and captain of the football team. Me, I had to bribe my skinny cousin Arturo to be my escort for the Grand March, and he only agreed after I signed a piece of paper and sealed it with a drop of blood from my index finger that I would do his Saturday morning paper route for a whole year! Man, that was the longest night of my life.

It wasn't over with the quinceañera, either, not by a long shot. My sister Czarina María Elena was voted Queen of the May by the faculty at our Catholic high school because she got good grades not only in her studies, but in her attitude and comportment — and because she was a teacher's pet. She got to wear a white velvet gown and a blue velvet cape just like the statue of the Virgin Mary in the side chapel of the cathedral. They had a big procession with a hundred little flower girls strewing rose petals in the aisles and a full choir and incense. My sister got to crown the Virgin Mary (who is also the Queen of the May). Even the Bishop attended. My sister got her picture in *Arizona Catholic Lifetime*, which is mailed to all the Catholics in town once a month. Were my Mamá and Papá proud!

During her senior year she was chosen Homecoming Queen, probably because Xavier was her steady boyfriend by then. She wore his letter sweater, which meant they were engaged to be engaged or something. The sweater had four gold stripes and a big "S" on it with a football, basketball, and baseball appliquéd on. I would have killed to have had that sweater!

It all happened in the same year, and boy, did Mamá sweat it out at that antique sewing machine. Whir, whir, clackety, clack, snip, snip. The treadle went so fast that her feet were a blur, and the little spools of thread danced so crazily on the spindle they looked like they would fly right off. Mamá was lost in layers and layers of velvet and tulle and organdy and dotted swiss and taffeta until you could barely see the top of her head, like some people buried in an avalanche I saw once in *National Geographic*.

And now Czarina María Elena is getting married — to Xavier, natch. She didn't want Mamá to make her dress or the bridesmaids' dresses because she wanted something modish and elaborate. I think Mamá was crestfallen at first and then later relieved when she realized how monumental the task would have been. We had to go to Phoenix to buy my sister's wedding dress because there was nothing in Tucson at Steinfeld's or Jácome's or Barbara's Bridal Fashions that suited her.

I had to go along on the trip, of course, since I'm going to be the maid of honor — because I'm her only sister, and Mamá says so, and besides, I'm still a virgin. But it doesn't stop there. She's going to have madrinas[4] of this and that — madrina de laso and madrina de arras and matron of honor — eight attendants in all, not counting the ringbearer and the flower girls.

It was boring going to so many department stores and bridal boutiques, flipping through magazines, trying on all those dresses that make you look like a Dairy Queen cone with eyes. Sure enough, my sister picked out something for me in a peach color that makes me look sallow, with turquoise for the madrinas, and satin shoes dyed to match for everyone. Personally, I think the wedding dress she picked makes her look like the Taj Mahal with hair. And me? I look like the Pyramid of the Sun at Teotihuacán, with legs. I started to protest, but Mamá gave me a look — how does she make her right eyebrow go into a "V" like that? So I kept my peace and didn't complain because Mamá likes everything to be nice and wonderful and peaceful and beautiful all the time in her little kingdom, world without end. Amen.

[4] bridesmaids

La Bailarina

The Dancer

All I ever really wanted to be was a dancer — a ballerina — the kind that gets all dressed up in something white and frothy with feathers and see-through veils and white silk stockings and white satin toe shoes and a paste-jewel crown. A ballerina is always a beautiful, sad princess who has ladies-in-waiting with flowers in their hair dancing around her. She's rescued from the witch in black by a handsome prince who leaps and twirls and throws her in the air and carries her upside down (she doesn't seem to mind), and nobody ever falls down.

The people who come to see you dance the ballet are real fancy. We went to see *Swan Lake* at the Temple of Music and Art on a school field trip once. The men wore tuxedos and top hats, and the ladies wore long dresses with white gloves and ropes of fake pearls. They had stoles made out of dead foxes and rabbits with little staring glass eyes, some with their tails still attached. The concert hall was painted all in gilt, and there was a red velvet curtain with gold tassels and a crystal chandelier as big as our house. It was all very high class.

But when I asked Papá about classical ballet lessons, he said, "No seas simple. They don't give lessons like that on our side of town, and who do you think is going to be chauffeuring you three times a week to the East Side Ballet Academy? Your Mamá doesn't drive, and I'm moonlighting at Blackie's Service Station. Anyway, those kind of dance lessons are for rich güeritas, and you'd be out of place."

He gave me a big smile and a hug, but I didn't feel any better.

"Okay, okay," I persisted. "What about tap-dancing lessons? They have classes after school at the "Y" on Third Avenue, and they're real cheap, and I can take the bus. My friend Graciela gets to go, and she says it's real fun. The shoes are neat — black patent leather tied with a ribbon at the ankle, with taps on the heel and toe so you clack-clack whenever you walk, and sometimes they make little sparks when you're dancing."

"No seas ridícula," he countered. "There's no way I'm going to give you permission to take those tap-dancing lessons and wear a skintight leotard — que no tiene vergüenza la juventud[1] — and those short skirts that when you twirl around enseñan todo, hasta los calzoncillos y las nalgas.[2] My compadre told me he went to a recital to see his niece, your friend Graciela, and the girls were all wearing pancake makeup and blue

[1] Young people, they have no shame.
[2] They show everything, even your undies and your butt.

eyeshadow and bright red lipstick, and they all looked like you know what. Excuse me, but that's what he said. What would your abuelita say? She'd probably have an ataque and keel right over from the susto and escándalo."

"Okay, okay," I tried. "What about flamenco? Father Estanislao's old aunt is visiting from Spain and is giving lessons in the parish hall after choir practice. It's free, and the girls wear long, flouncy dresses and three petticoats and a mantilla and shawl even. Abuelita would like that. There's not much showing off, either; they just stand in one spot and do the zapateado and click those castanets."

"Ahora sí," said Papá. "Now you're going to start getting ideas that you're española. Stay true to your culture. You're mexicana through and through. Besides, I don't want you hanging around those gachupines who conquered our fatherland and destroyed our temples and stole our gold and silver, y que se creen con todo eso de lo gitano y fandango y jota."[3]

So, get this. Angel Hernández and Mercedes Guerrero opened up El Instituto del Ballet Folklórico Mexicano last year on West Drachman Street. What I wouldn't give to wear one of those trajes de gala from Jalisco and dance "La Negra"; or el traje de jarocha from Vera Cruz, a white lace dress with an embroidered apron and silk-fringed rebozo, and dance "La Bamba"; or a china poblana dress from Puebla, with the eagle and the serpent and the Mexican flag appliquéd in sequins, and dance "La Espuelas de Amazoc."

[3] who think they're superior with all those Spanish airs

But I'm too old — I'm in my early thirties now — and I'd feel ridiculous clomping around with all those quinceañeras.[4]

I can remember my great-grandmother Cleofas dancing "El Jarabe Tapatío" on her saint's day in the back lot at my grandmother's house in Barrio Hollywood. She'd gather up her long, black, homespun skirt and dance barefooted in the dusty corral, her wide Indian feet pounding the earth into little explosions of dirt. She'd hum the tune through the gaps in her teeth, her huge gold filigree coqueta earrings weighing down her earlobes almost to her shoulders, her thin white braids whipping the air. She used to tell me, in her Nahuatl-laced Spanish, her ancient face wrinkling in delight, how as a young girl she had been a calentano dancer in her village of Pungarabato and kept time to the music while her feet tapped out the rhythm on a hollow log called a tarimba while the conjunto de Juan Reynoso played "El Son Guerrense."

So I guess it's in my blood.

Anyway, I'm married now with one kid and another one on the way. Now don't get me wrong — I'm crazy about my husband and child. But my viejo used to take me dancing all the time when we were novios. I'd get all dressed up in a red lace dress and red high heels, and tirábamos la chancla[5] every Saturday night at El Casino Ballroom or Club La Selva on West Congress Street. We'd dance every dance, and the little circles

---

[4] 15-year-old debutantes

[5] danced a lot (literally, "threw our shoes")

of light would be going around and around on the ceiling, and I was so happy that sometimes I felt that I wasn't even on this earth.

But now he usually says he's too tired, pobre viejo, working full time and going to the university at night; he's got to study. Or there's a football game on TV or a pickup basketball game with his buddies at La Madera Park.

No matter.

It's just that sometimes when the baby is crying and I'm standing at the kitchen sink, my hands chapped from the dishwater, my face sweaty from the steam, my legs achy from standing so long to cashier the afternoon shift at ABCO to make ends meet . . .

I think I'm gonna get those red high heels that I have in a box on the shelf at the back of our bedroom closet, and I'm just going to waltz right out of here . . .

for a little while.

La Tortillera

The Tortilla Maker

Casa donde no hay harina, todo se hace remolina.[1]

There are a few things I must explain about my mother. She has an inborn and natural elegance and grace, a genetic exquisiteness. People turn their heads and stare in admiration when she walks by. I have spent most of my life following a few paces behind her, pretending to carry the train of an imagined magnificent gossamer cape.

She is regal. And there is no place where she reigns more absolutely than in the Kingdom of the Kitchen. There she has decreed irrevocable laws with monarchical absoluteness. There she is the queen and I, alas, the court jester.

---

[1] In the house where there is no flour, everything will turn to shambles. (Where there is no discipline, all will be lost.)

These are the Laws of the Kitchen:

Law Number 1: Tamales are not made; they are sculpted.

Law Number 2: Sopa is not soup; it is "the lovely broth."

Law Number 3: One must always wear an apron when embarking on a kitchen mission. The apron must be handmade and embroidered with the days of the week (preferably in cross-stitch), and the correct one must be worn each day.

Law Number 4: A dining table must always have a starched and ironed cloth — never, never placemats.

Law Number 5: Tortillas are the essence of life, the symbol of eternity, the circle that is unbroken, the shortest distance between two points.

Law Number 6: Law Number 5 takes precedence over laws number one through four and the Six Precepts of the Roman Catholic Church.

Law Number 7: The unfortunates who buy their tortillas from the supermarket, wrapped in plastic, might as well move to Los Angeles, for they have already lost their souls.

A day in the kitchen with my mother is an oft-repeated disaster echoing past scenarios:

"Patricia, es lástima that you don't make homemade tortillas more often. Pobres de tus criaturas.[2] Do you want your niños

---

[2] Your poor children

to grow up without culture and underprivileged? How can you expect them to know the meaning of life?"

"You are right, Mamá. I just don't ever seem to have the time. And anyway, they never seem to come out right. One time I forgot to put in the baking powder, and they were as hard as soda crackers. The next time I put in too much baking powder, and they puffed up like balloons. They're either too salty or too bland. Sometimes I add too much water, and they have the consistency of glue, or not enough, and they are like rubber. And when I try to roll them out, they're shaped funny."

"That's all right, mihijta. You are here today, and you have the time, so let's make them together. I'll go through it with you [for the hundredth time] step by step." (An audible sigh.)

"Well, Mamacita, it would be most helpful if you would give me some measuring spoons and cups. We could measure the ingredients, and then I could write down all the amounts, and then perhaps when I made them at home [wishful thinking] they would turn out better."

"Measure? Who needs to measure? You can feel it in your alma if the amounts are right. Your heart will tell you. See? I cup my hand like this, and I know it's enough baking powder. The flour — just make a lovely snowy mound of it in the middle of the bowl. And add the salt in the form of La Santa Cruz to bless the bread. Don't worry. La Virgen de Guadalupe will guide you."

(I have already broken one of her favorite china cups during our morning coffee session. There is a stain of my scrambled egg glowing fluorescently on her white linen tablecloth with the crocheted hem. She has told me three times to lower my voice and put on an apron — the one that says "martes." She always has a candle burning for me on her bedroom altar with its army of saints, virgins, Santos Niños, and Almighty Poderosos. Her intentions are unspecified, but I think it has something to do with the fact that I cook with frozen food and use paper napkins.)

She pours, spoons, sifts, stirs, mixes, and kneads with grace and deliberation. I watch with feigned interest and intensity. I am thinking about the tortillas at the supermarket in the plastic wrappers. The candle on the little altar flares and dies out.

The dough is ready. Now we must make little bolitas of perfectly uniform masa that must "rest" for half an hour under a cross-stitched embroidered cloth that says "Tortillas."

It is now time to roll the tortillas out. We take the cloth off ceremoniously. Mamá's bolitas of masa have expanded into symmetrical mounds of dough. Mine, however, are lumpy and misshapen.

Mamá: Now we will roll them out. I will let you use the palote[3] that my father made for me when I was but a little girl of six. Have I ever told you the story of how I began making tortillas for our family of eight when I was so small that I used to have to stand on a wooden box to reach the counter?

---

[3] rolling pin

"Yes, Mamá." This story has been so often recited that it has become part of our family folklore with mythic importance equal to Popocatépetl and Ixtacihuatl.

"You roll them out gently. Now watch," Mamá demonstrates. "Put your right foot forward so that your body will be balanced in its weight as you lean forward to roll out the dough. That will ensure that the tortilla will be uniform." (And, incidentally, my life.)

The sweat is forming on my upper lip. I take the palote in my right hand, arrange my feet as directed, and try to roll out the dough into the shape of a circle. The masa has a mind of its own. It resists, gathers strength, overpowers and subdues me.

Mamá comments with a patient sigh, "That doesn't look too bad, mihijta. It is not quite round, it's true, but let's cook it and see how it comes out."

She places my Rorschach tortilla on the comal. It energizes with the heat. It browns, it puffs, it grows appendages, it hardens. The morning's lesson progresses. My stack of tortillas grows at a precarious tilt, a leaning tower of confusion. I am dusted with white flour from head to foot. My fingernails are luminous with dough. I am exhausted.

Mamá announces with pious finality, "There. Now we're done. That was not so hard, now was it? Children! Come and see the tortillas your mother has made!"

From the mouths of little children: "Your tortillas look funny, Mom! How come they don't look like Nani's? That one looks like a rabbit. That one looks like a mushroom. That one looks like Florida! And that one looks like Texas!"

It wouldn't be so bad, I suppose, if one of them had been shaped like the state of Chihuahua. But Texas is unacceptable.

Mamacita relights the candle to St. Jude, the patron of hopeless cases.

A la mejor cocinera se le ahuma la olla.[4]

---

[4] Even the best cook can burn the pot. (No one is perfect.)

Plumas

Feathers

Banish care; if there are bounds to pleasure, the saddest life must also have an end. Then weave the chaplet of flowers, and sing thy songs in praise of the all-powerful God; for the glory of this world soon fadeth away. Rejoice in the green freshness of thy Spring; for the day will come when thou shalt sigh for these joys in vain; when the sceptre shall pass from thy hands, thy servants desolate in thy courts, thy sons, and the sons of thy nobles shall drink the dregs of distress, and all the pomp of thy victories and triumphs shall live only in their recollection. . . . The goods of this life, its glories and its riches, are but lent to us, its substance is but an illusory shadow, and the things of today shall change on the coming of the morrow. Then gather the fairest flowers from thy gardens, to bind round thy brow, and seize the joys of the present, ere they perish.

—Nezahualcoyotl, Aztec emperor and poet king

William Prescott, *The Conquest of Mexico*

Paloma Flores stepped nimbly off of the 7:00 A.M. crosstown bus at the corner of Glenn and Palo Verde Streets. She was a few minutes late for work as usual, and she walked hurriedly through the chain-link fence that led past the football field to the high school parking lot. She darted among the parked cars as fast as her slender muscular legs and sensible shoes could carry her. When she reached the "Employees Only" entrance at the back of the brick cafeteria building, she ran up the concrete steps, fumbled with her key, and opened the heavy, steel security door slowly. She was careful not to close it too noisily lest her tardiness be noticed. The supervisor of the cafeteria staff, Sister Fredericka, was a stout German nun with a ruddy face, a quick temper, and a strident voice. She ran the kitchen with the military precision of boot camp and maintained the discipline with religious fervor. She tolerated no lapses in punctuality, efficiency, cleanliness, or order. The last thing that Paloma Flores wanted was any extra attention from Sor Fredericka or a scolding from her in her thick Teutonic tongue.

Paloma Flores hung her plain, gray cloth coat on a hook in the staff lounge and slipped a clean white smock from the bin of freshly laundered linen over her shapeless cotton frock. She then carefully stretched a hairnet over her thickly braided tresses — her hair was ebony, radiant, but she wore it modestly in a sleeping coil on top of her elegant head. Over the hairnet she drew a cap of fine gauze to ensure that every strand was in place and tucked out of sight. It was a health department requirement, and any errant lock would be scrutinized by Sister

Fredericka until she matched it with its hapless owner. Then she would mark demerits next to the guilty party's name in the little black book that she carried in the oversized pockets of her black smock. Ten demerits and one's pay could be docked; too many demerits and one could be dismissed.

Paloma Flores slipped as quietly and unobtrusively as possible into the work line at the stainless-steel counters in the cafeteria kitchen. Her coworkers, all women, chattered in Spanish as they worked — chop, chop; slice, slice; stir, stir. Plática y plática:[1] of sweethearts and husbands and children and friends and in-laws; of fears and illnesses and remedies; of love and disillusionment; of recipes and herbs and fashion and fiestas. Plática y plática; mincing onions, plática; cubing meat, plática; peeling carrots and potatoes, plática; kneading dough, plática.

Paloma Flores had become accustomed to the good-natured teasing about her tardiness from her work companions — the curious glances, the questioning raised eyebrows, the knowing smirks — especially from Carmen García, who stood opposite her at the work counter. Carmen seemed out of place in the cafeteria kitchen assembly line with her pompadour, enormous dangling earrings made of peacock feathers, stiletto heels, false eyelashes, and exotic perfume. She was a sharp contrast to plain and unadorned Paloma Flores. But Carmen had a heart of gold and meant well. She was determined simply to draw out

[1] chatter; gossip; conversation

the shy and reticent Paloma, who was the only one of the women who rarely spoke or shared any details with her companions about her solitary life.

"Late again?" Carmen García would tease when Sor Fredericka, her oversized rosary beads rattling on her waist, had passed out of earshot on her inspection tour. "What's going on? Do you have a boyfriend that you're keeping a secret from us? Is someone hiding under your bed who makes you late?"

Paloma Flores' nimble fingers never faltered in their culinary tasks as she endured Carmen's good-natured ribbing with a quiet smile and a flush on her cheeks. She kept her silence; she had no choice. How could she tell them about the dream?

The recurrent dream startled her bolt upright in her narrow, single bed in her modest, neat room in the boarding house of Doña Amparito on Convent Street. The dream left her wide-eyed and sleepless, her heart pounding, her forehead damp with excitement, her lungs choking with a perfumed smoke, her body trembling, her ears ringing with the faraway haunting sound of drums and flutes and conch shells.

The massive oak clock at the far end of the cafeteria ticked off the minutes brassily — countdown to the lunch hour and the swarm of noisy, hungry teenagers who would invade the dining hall at precisely 12:05 P.M. The echo of the ticking clock was lost in the din of students scraping chairs, banging trays and utensils, slurping milk and juice, and chattering in excited, high-pitched voices. They were as hungry and efficient as locusts, and it would not be long before the cafeteria was again quiet, the horde of adolescents surging out the double-wide glass doors onto the school grounds.

The kitchen staff, famished by now, would hurriedly eat lunch — the leftovers of today's menu, the fruit of their own labors. Then the clamor and chatter would begin again: plática, plática; the clink of glasses and clatter of plates and utensils, plática; the racket of metal pots and pans, plática; the rattle of plastic trays, plática; the steam rising from the hot, sudsy wash and rinse water like the vapors from an ancient volcano. Then the cafeteria workers — their backs aching, their feet tired and swollen from standing at their labors, their hands reddened — would ebb out the back door and surge like a wave across the parking lot en route to the shores of their own private lives.

Carmen García removed the detested hairnet and gauze cap and placed a bright-green bandanna over her pompadour to protect her hairdo from the fickle breezes. She tied a knot under her chin and touched up her lipstick, rouge, and cologne. "Okay, Paloma," she teased, "now don't be late tomorrow or you might get caught by Sister Fredericka. Boy, I sure would like to meet this novio of yours; I'll bet he's quite a looker. Maybe I should steal him from you!" She smiled a wide grin, her gold-capped teeth glinting. They strolled together through the parking lot until they reached Carmen's vintage Chevrolet. Carmen blew rings of smoke out her heart-shaped "Cherries in the Snow" mouth, then tapped the ashes from her cigarette with her long, red fingernails that shone like jewels in the sun.

"Anyway, Honey," she added as she struggled with the car door, "you can always talk to me and let me know what's really going on." Paloma Flores' cheeks reddened, but she kept her counsel.

Her name was Xochitl, which meant "flower bird" in Nahuatl. She was a Cihuateopixque, a female priest dedicated to the Aztec goddess Tonantzín, the creator goddess, the earth and harvest goddess, the goddess of young growth and beauty.

Xochitl wore her midnight-black hair long to her waist, free and flowing, and the locks were interlaced with strips of colored cloth and feathers. Her face was decorated with red, yellow, and white paint and her breasts, arms, and shoulders were perfumed with a liquid amber called *isataisatahte*. Attached to her waist was a thick, black strap anointed with a sweet-smelling balsam. In her right hand she carried an enormous burden basket of fragrant herbs and flowers, for spring was the time for the offering of flowers to Tonantzín.

In her left hand Xochitl carried a fan of feathers and a little flag of beaten gold topped with the feathers of the macaw. She wore earplugs of coral and jade, a necklace of gold with pearls and amethysts, and bracelets and anklets of gold, turquoise, and emeralds that were trimmed in feathers. Her lower lip was pierced and set with pieces of rock crystal, within which were stuck blue feathers of the hummingbird that made them seem like sapphires. She wore these ornaments hanging as if they came out of her flesh, and she also had golden half-moons hanging from her lips. Her nose was pierced and therein was inserted fine turquoise. Her sandals were of jaguar fur adorned with gold and precious stones; the thongs were of gold thread embellished with trogon feathers from the deep forests.

She had a crown of feathers called a *tlauhquecholtzontli*, which was made of the feathers of the roseate spoonbill. She wore it with the *thauhquecholeuatl*, a jacket of spoonbill feathers, and the *tzapocueitl*, a petticoat of green feathers from the Quetzal bird. The garments lapped over one another like tiles. In addition, she wore a headband called the *quetzalallapiloni*, an adornment of beaten gold with the feathers of the Quetzal bird.

She ascended the thousand steps to the summit of the pyramid where the altar of Tonantzín was located. Xochitl was attended by a hundred vestal virgins who chanted solemnly. At the summit awaited a score of priests. Their bodies were horrible with tattoos, their faces covered with the *coa-xayacacatl*, the snake mask of mosaic turquoise. The priests were resplendent in feather headdresses and capes of brilliant plumage. They carried in their right hands the *chicahuaztlei*, an elaborately carved staff adorned with feathers and bells. Around their waists they wore hooves, fruit, shells, and cocoons, and dried nuts, seashells, bones, and metal bells were strung on a string sewn to a leather band that was decorated with feathers.

A hundred brazier fires were burning, and an incense called copal ascended in fragrant clouds to the starlit heavens. Exceedingly large drums were brilliantly painted and bedecked with gold bands and gay feather ornaments, and they were elaborately carved with the reliefs of the eagle and jaguar warriors.

69

There were many other drums made of all manner of snake and animal skins, tortoise and armadillo shells, and horns, flutes, and conch shells.

The singing and the chanting of the priests, the music from the instruments, the rhythms and swaying of the dancing attendants, the crackling of the fires and the roar of the winds, the sound of it all together was so haunting that it seemed to be a sound from the very center of the earth. One could hear it at a distance of twenty leagues, and it was said that it could wake those in the deepest slumber. Even the dead.

Chop, chop. Slice, slice. Stir, stir. Plática, plática. The women are busy at their kitchen stations, their foreheads furrowed, their heads bent in concentration. There is an empty space at the workspace opposite Carmen García. Paloma Flores has not been to work for over a week. She has sent no word. Her phone goes unanswered, her mail returned.

Chop, chop. Slice, slice. Plática, plática. "So, Carmen, what ever happened to la Paloma?" asks a concerned Doña Antoñita, a gray-haired grandmother of six who is working diligently at the station next to Carmen. "Why isn't she coming to work anymore? She hasn't been in for days."

Carmen García pauses, then flutters her hands excitedly and fingers her brooch made of butterfly wings. "I'm not sure I know exactly what's going on." She leans over dramatically and speaks in a voice a little louder than a whisper. There is silence in the assembly line as the cooks pause at their tasks, their utensils suspended in midair, straining to hear every word. "I heard that she was fired by la Sister Fredericka and won't be coming back."

"Ay, pobre, for heaven's sakes, why?" asks Doña Antoñita. "Tan buena y tan trabajadora."[2]

Carmen's false eyelashes flutter like fans, but her eyes shine with a flame dark and deep. "Yeah, I know," she says sympathetically. "It's too bad. But I guess la Sister got mad or something. I overheard her saying something to the fry cook, something about how she just couldn't tolerate it. Rules are rules. Something about she had never in all her years seen anything like it. Something about how Paloma's feathers kept getting in the soup."

---

[2] So good and such a good worker.

La Virgen de la Soledad

The Virgin of Loneliness

The crumbling rock shrine of La Virgen de la Soledad at the top of the hill overlooking the Sierra Encantada Guest Ranch and Spa is a favorite mecca of the colorfully clad, camera-laden tourists who come to winter in the southern Arizona desert, far from the inclement weather of the Midwest and East. There is, of course, a story that goes with the shrine, but like so much southwestern history, it has been embellished and distorted with the passage of time and the telling. An "official" version of the legend of the grotto has been published in the guest ranch brochure, the owners of the resort wishing to capitalize on any appeal that guests might find in the romance of the past.

The brochure reads:

Dolores Cárdenas de Romero (1865-1885), to whom this shrine is dedicated (and which is now on the register of historic places), was the first wife of Don Estéban Romero, the original owner of the Sierra Encantada Ranch. She died tragically and unexpectedly in the bloom of her youth, having contracted a mysterious malady. When she became ill, she was moved to the Convent of San Cosme on the banks of the Santa Cruz River in Tucson, where she was cared for by the good sisters. In spite of their attention and prayers, she wasted and succumbed to the ravages of her illness on her twentieth birthday.

The Sierra Encantada Guest Ranch and Spa is an isolated cattle ranch founded more than a century ago beside a perennial stream in the Tanque Verde Draw between the Santa Catalina and Rincón Mountains on the far east side of Tucson. It was sold in the fifties to enterprising Anglo investors by the fourth-generation descendants of Don Estéban Romero, one of the most illustrious pioneers of the Pimería Alta. He was fabled for his blood lines, his good looks, his prize cattle, his business acumen, and his way with women and horses.

Don Estéban's great-great-grandson, Don Gorgonio Romero, now a septuagenarian, was the caretaker of a weathered, leather, antique trunk that was peeling in curling strips from exposure to the elements. It contained precious family memorabilia and various family documents, including Dolores Cárdenas de Romero's small velvet-bound diary tied with a tattered white ribbon. But her fine flowing script has faded on the disintegrating yellowing paper and is no longer legible. Don Gorgonio remembered the history of the shrine up until a few years ago, but alas, no one recorded the story, and as Don Gorgonio's mind has failed along with his body in recent years, attempts to revive his memory have been unsuccessful.

Tucson is a Sun Belt city that prides itself on growth, progress, and appreciating land values. It is only a matter of time before the Sierra Encantada Guest Ranch will be bought and subdivided by developers in their inexorable march east to the mountains. But for the present at least, the hundred remaining acres of the rancho, a small remnant of Don Estéban's familial legacy, act as a buffer from the encroaching urban sprawl of townhouses, shopping malls, service stations, and golf courses. It is a nationally and internationally renowned haven where the city-weary, world-weary traveler and businessperson can "get away from it all" in the purple and blue shadows of the saguaro- and star-studded mountains.

The spacious, well-kept grounds of the Sierra Encantada Guest Ranch, which has earned five stars in a famous travel guide, contains stables, a swimming pool and spa, tennis courts, and numerous tile-roofed casitas and apartments painted in the pastel desert hues that are so much in vogue. The casitas are strategically placed on the grounds for maximum privacy and offer the romantic ambiance of Old Mexico with, of course, telephones, cable television, microwave ovens, and room service.

Of the original hacienda, there remains only the main ranch house, the chapel, an old stone well filled with debris, century-old mesquite retaque corrals, and a small isolated Romero family cemetery hidden in an aromatic mesquite grove about half a mile from the ranch headquarters.

The ancient ranch house, which bears a lintel inscribed with the date 1850, has multiple fireplaces, thick adobe walls, and saguaro-ribbed ceilings. It has been renovated and updated with impeccable taste and now serves as an office, library, TV lounge, and dining room for the distinguished guests. There is an air of historical authenticity and gentility about the place that the glittering, modern destination resorts in the foothills of the Santa Catalina Mountains lack.

The small adobe chapel, which is down a flagstone pathway around the swimming pool, is but a stone's throw from the main ranch house. It was built under the guidance of the frail Dolores Cárdenas de Romero. It once was fragrant with blossoms from her rose gardens, the aroma of melting candle wax and incense, and the perfumed breath of her supplications. Now the chapel is redolent with the smells of cigarette smoke, peanuts, pretzels, beer, and other libations. A flickering neon sign with a lasso-throwing, bronco-riding cowboy in silhouette is suspended from the small bell tower of the chapel. "Rosita's Cantina," it announces. The bell, which once called the faithful from the neighboring ranchos to gather when the saintly padre arrived from town to say mass, to baptize, and to marry, has long since been removed, and it now hangs from the portico of the dining hall to call the guests to breakfast, lunch, dinner, and cocktails. In the dim shadows of the ancient capilla,[1] the click of pool balls has replace the click of silver and crystal rosary beads, and raucous laughter, conversation, and the clink of glasses drown

[1] chapel

out the prayerful echoes of the people's alabanzas and Dolores' litanies and lamentations.

The venerable monument and cross-strewn camposanto of the Romero family contains three dozen or so graves of Don Estéban's descendants, including the final resting place of the illustrious pioneer himself, his three wives (all of whom he managed to outlive), numerous offspring, and the blessed bones of his faithful ranch hands and their families.

The camposanto is a little off the beaten path of the main tourist facilities; one might expect that it would have been forgotten or neglected. Not so. In the custom of the pious and faithful mexicano, Don Gorgonio and his family and dozens of other descendants of Don Estéban make a pilgrimage each year to the burial place of their ancestors. They have a simple mass said and recite the glorious mysteries of the rosary on the 2nd of November, El Día de los Muertos. Then they pay further homage to the souls of their dear departed by cleaning, repairing, and decorating the graves with jars of fresh flowers and candles that have been blessed with holy water.

The cemetery has also become a focus of curiosity for some of the guests who are charmed by the quaintness and antiquity of Mexican customs. They join the family as onlookers, meditating on the fragility of life and all its ephemeral pomp under the lacy mantillas of the mesquite trees. They then embellish the collapsing mounds with small souvenirs of their visit — for good luck. The grave that receives the most tokens is that of Dolores Cárdenas de Romero — the child bride and first wife of Don Estéban, who died without producing him an heir.

77

But by far the most popular destination of the tourist pilgrims is the aforementioned shrine of La Virgen de la Soledad, which the grieving and shocked Don Estéban built in memory of his beautiful tormented wife. The shrine, embellished by polished stones from the creek that shine in the sun, is located on the western slope of a small rock-strewn hillside facing the ranch. It is only a leisurely fifteen-minute stroll from the house on a path that the groundskeeper (himself a descendent of one of Don Estéban's faithful vaqueros) keeps cleared, lest a careless or infirm vacationer trip and fall. It is a popular morning excursion after the sumptuous brunches. There the guests and an occasional visitor from town light candles and make wishes to the ever-vigilant Virgin in the rock grotto. The statue of La Virgen de la Soledad is weathered and cracked — a victim of time and the seasons — and the original paint had long since faded and peeled off. But the statue is miraculously intact in spite of its age and periodic acts of vandalism. Generations of melted wax and silver milagros[2] have been left by the supplicants, and they add to the supernatural ambiance of the shrine. It is said if you light a candle and it burns all night without blowing out, you will find true love.

La Virgen de la Soledad, laden with the secret entreaties of so many, gazes serenely down at the sun-baked tourists and the ever-flickering candles that they light in the hopeful notion that their dreams and prayers will be fulfilled by the intercession of the soul of Dolores Cárdenas de Romero, who wasted

[2] small gift to a saint depicting object for which a miracle is sought

away of tristeza y melancolía in the year of the Great Drought—
of the desert and of her womb.

The Diary

It has not rained for fifteen months. My husband, Don Estéban,
speaks little these days, and only in monosyllables, or answers
my questions with a clipped sí o no. He is gone from sunup to
sundown, roaming the canyons to count the bloated corpses of
his prize herd that lie scattered like giant raisins in the sere and
browned hills. He and his vaqueros arrive at the rancho long
after it is dark with a few scraggly cattle in tow. They draw
water for the crazed and bulging-eyed survivors from the black
scummy depths of the ever-receding well.

My husband and his vaqueros eat the meal in silence that I
have prepared for them. Holding the steaming cups of coffee in
both hands, they speak only to tally the day's losses or to plan
the next day's foray. I stand in the kitchen door, watchful,
obedient, waiting for a word or a gesture to banish my loneliness. Nothing.

The vaqueros wipe their hands and mouths on their sleeves,
scrape their chairs on the pine floor, and, spurs jingling, retire
to the bunkhouse. Don Estéban finishes his supper, pushes his
plate away listlessly, and goes silently into the sala to read or
brood by the light of the kerosene lamp. I will wait for him in
our moonlit bed, lulled by the coyote's lament, my hands folded
in prayer on my empty womb. When I awake to the first rays of
the sun, he is gone.

The garden by my kitchen window was my haven. From the stone well I drew buckets of crystal water to nourish the sweet and loamy earth. Herbs and flowers and roses once perfumed the air of my oasis. I am barren, but my garden was fertile and bountiful. With my songs the seedlings grew, pregnant with flowers and fruit. But now the well water is too dear, and my garden has burned and shriveled in the drying winds. My only companions are the flies, buzzing incessantly in the suspended air, oblivious to the heat and death rising like a miasma from the low-lying hills.

My husband notices that I am frail. I have taken to pacing and wringing my hands, watching for the rain-laden clouds to come over purple mountains. "Let me take you in the buckboard to town. This is no place for a woman," he says. But I prefer to be here, alone, keeping my vigil. I must wait for the rains to quicken me. I do not want to suffer the inquiring glances and raised eyebrows of the clucking women. "¿Todavía no?" They pat my abdomen maternally.

"Todavía no."

"You have to make a manda. The Virgin is the answer. La Virgen embarazada[3] will come to your aid and answer your prayers."

The Virgin, yes. La Virgen embarazada. Daily I kneel on the sharp stones of the arroyo until my knees bleed. The rocks are iridescent with the melted wax of my candles. The leaves of the cottonwood and aliso trees sway with the breath of my sighs.

---

[3] the pregnant Virgin

La Virgen, yes, I see her now. Her mantle is the blue and burning sky. Her crown is the sun. Her smile is the pale gibbous moon, her hair the wisps of false clouds. Her arms are the lengthening shadows that beckon me to the west. She makes me promises — if only I will bring her flowers.

La Creciente

The Flood

El que vive en la memoria nunca muere.[1]

I had just danced the last dance with Teodoro Sánchez. He had come to the Salazar family reunion on the east end of Aravaipa Canyon from Mammoth on the west end. He had journeyed by mule on the old mining road — across the San Pedro River, up over the draw past Copper Creek to Table Mountain, where he could see Holy Joe Peak shimmering in the distance, down Turkey Creek, past the prehistoric cliff dwellings near Bear Creek. He had forded Aravaipa Creek three times. "Me bauticé tres veces,"[2] he informed me solemnly. He scoffed at us third- and fourth-generation city slickers in our pickup campers, four-wheel-drive vehicles, and motor homes who had driven east to

---

[1] The person who lives in our memory never dies.

[2] I was baptized three times.

Willcox on the interstate and then had caravanned and complained on the fifty miles of washed-out, potted, dirt road north from Willcox, through Bonita and the Sulfur Springs Valley. It had taken us three hours to reach the ancient orchard on the Salazar family homestead on Aravaipa Creek; it had taken Teodoro Sánchez two days.

He had been companion to the eagle, to the gray hawk, to the coyote and the mountain lion, to the bighorn sheep and the deer. He had slept under the sky beneath billowing cumulus clouds and the constellations. He smelled of chaparral and mesquite pollen and agave blooms and mesa dust and stream bottom and the bone dust of generations.

As we circled the dance floor, he would doff his hat occasionally in the direction of his travel companion, the faithful mule whom he had christened Lola — "because she sings so pretty," he said. Lola was tethered to a venerable streamside sycamore and was grazing placidly next to his campsite — a fire ring, a charred coffee pot, a frying pan, a faded serape, and a yellow rain slicker hanging from a branch of the tree. It was what he called home for the long weekend of festivities.

"Do you know why I prefer a mule over a horse?" he asked me over the din of music as he skidded in time to the corrido and swayed his narrow hips. He pulled me close to him by the waist and shouted in my ear, "'Cause my grandpa used to tell me that they're better than a horse. They work harder, they don't eat as much, they live longer, and they're smarter. And prettier." He grinned his wide perfect grin and laughed, his laughter riding the summer breeze to the tops of the trees, his mestizo face gleaming in the moonlight like polished mahogany.

"That's what my Tata Sánchez used to say. And my Tata knew horses, mules, and women." A guffaw. A zapateado.[3] A grito. He threw his hat into the air, and it spiraled down over the heads of the dancers. "¡Qué viva México! ¡Qué vivan los Salazares y los Sánchez y todos los paisanos mexicanos de Aravaipa!"

We had not missed a dance except for the special one dedicated to the widow, Doña Rosalía Sálazar de Whelan, the only surviving child of Don Epimenio and Doña Crespina Sálazar, the original settlers in El Cañón. The band played with the waltz "Sobre Las Olas" and we all — three hundred strong — formed a reverent circle around Dona Rosalía as she abandoned her walking cane and her lawn chair and danced with her son-in-law, Roy Salge. Erect and still beautiful in spite of her eighty-nine years, Doña Rosalía was every inch the queen of the fiesta in her powder-blue dress with the wide lace collar, her white hair perfectly coiffed in a finger wave, her skin unwrinkled and translucent in the moonlight. Her sturdily clad feet kept time haltingly but unerringly and gracefully to the music. Her eyes were dreamy with the memories of another time, other arms, another dear face.

We decided to pass the hat for El Conjunto de los Amigos so that they would play for a couple more hours. They had been playing their hearts out — two guitars, a bass, two violins, and

[3] tapping one's feet in time to the music

85

an accordion doing corridos, cumbias, boleros, waltzes, and rock and roll. All of us revelers had crowded the wooden dance platform in the century-old orchard and field on the banks of Aravaipa Creek. We were stomping, sliding, and swaying to the rhythm of the little norteño band that had traveled the sixty miles from Safford to play for the gathering of descendants and friends of the Mexican pioneers who had settled in this arcadian valley decades ago.

Norma Tapia Luepke had strung an extension cord four hundred feet long from the generator by the chicken coop down the slope from her grandmother Victoria's adobe house. The dance platform was strung with party lights, but they paled in contrast to the harvest moon that now rose over the canyon walls, snagged on the massive red butte called La Chimenea, and illuminated us merrymakers until we danced with our own shadows.

There were no stars. Doña Luna tolerated no rivals in the midnight sky — except for the tiny fireflies that flickered in the groves of streamside willows and alders like a miniature galaxy in descendence. The moonbeams bounced off the canyon walls: the faces of the dancers were incandescent; the leaves of the giant cottonwood and sycamore trees glittered like green glass; and the unripened fruit in the ancient orchard shone like Christmas baubles.

Now it was midnight, and the moon hung heavily in the heavens, her huge yellow eye unblinking, watching the festivities. We were not ready to stop dancing, so when Victor Vásquez passed his well-worn Stetson, we filled it to the brim with ones and fives and tens. Grinning ear to ear, Victor returned to the bandstand, and the musicians began tuning their instruments amid shouts and hurrahs. We were ready to dance all night.

Then it happened without the slightest warning. The breeze that had been but a caressing summer zephyr was pushed down the slopes of the Pinaleño Mountains by a fast tropical storm from the Gulf of Mexico two thousand miles away. It swept down the Sulfur Springs and Aravaipa Valleys and gathered velocity at Four Mile Camp and at the old Whelan homestead at Dry Camp and at the Eureka Ranch and at the confluence of Aravaipa Creek. And then it blew downstream in powerful gusts that knocked the hats off of the gentlemen and lifted the skirts and unraveled the hairdos of the señoras and señoritas.

There was a thunderclap that rumbled in from the distant mountains, and then a towering thunderhead rode the upper-air currents over the mesas and canyon walls like a primeval galleon riding the ocean tides.

Then the eye of Doña Luna snapped shut.

Everything was thrown into pitch-black darkness as the deluge began. Everyone ran to their respective campsites, scrambling, grabbing ponchos and tarps and raincoats to ward off the pelting rain and stinging hail. Jagged threads of lightning stitched the canopy of the sky and alternately threw the fields into brilliant light and then darkness, illuminating with a pulsing eerie glow the groups of partygoers huddled beneath the enormous umbrellas of the trees.

Everyone ran, that is, except for Teodoro Sánchez, who stood in the middle of the fallow field and laughed, raising his face to the weeping sky.

It seemed but a few minutes before the gentle murmuring stream began to escape its banks and roll over the fields. It swallowed Norma's vegetable garden in a single gulp. The crystalline waters of the creek were darkened now with mud, sand, and creekside debris. The campsites were swamped: paper plates and plastic forks, tents and sleeping bags, coolers and grills were all swept away in the churning water. We escaped to higher ground near the road, and before our astonished eyes, the chicken coop sailed away around the bend with all feathered inhabitants — chickens, roosters, ducks, geese, and peacocks — squawking from the flimsy roof.

The thunderclaps continued their deafening rumble. The rain fell in torrents that blinded us. The creek continued to rise. We abandoned our campsites and vehicles to their wet fate and hurriedly moved from the roadside bank to the Salazar family cemetery on top of a boulder- and mesquite-studded mesa. Teodoro Sánchez had untethered his mule and ridden her to a small bluff overlooking the camposanto. There from our vantage point among the gravestones and the difuntitos,[4] we watched the flash flood through the curtain of rain.

Aravaipa Creek was swollen now with water from a hundred springs, creeks, rivulets, and arroyos. It roared past, carrying

[4] the deceased (affectionate)

88

whole sycamores, and cottonwood and walnut trees as big as barns, and fences, windmills, bottomland, tractors, cattle, and phantasmal objects indistinguishable in the downpour.

The lightning crackled. We rubbed our eyes with our fists to clear out the cataracts of mist. Then, disbelieving, we saw the ghostly form of Don Epimenio Sálazar, wizened at the age of 100, like an archetypal Noah, come sailing around the bend of the upper creek at the head of a phantom flotilla. He was standing in his floating ranch wagon holding the reins of his team of draw horses. The carreta was piled with tottering pyramids of the harvests of his orchards: his renowned apples, three kinds of pears, peaches and apricots, quince and plums. At his side was his wife, Doña Crespina, drifting by on her huge cast-iron stove, her face flushed from cooking. In her right hand she was balancing a tower of flour tortillas that reached to the tops of the bluffs, and in her left hand she held a teetering stack of cooking pans, crowned with the azafata brimming with her famous cinnamon-scented rice pudding. Cruising behind Don Epimenio and Doña Crespina, sitting on the roof of the boguecito with the fringed top, were six of their beautiful daughters, Pastora, Aurelia, Refugia, Lucia, Luisa, and Victoria. They were dressed in homespun dresses and aprons and were surrounded by sacks of dried chile, corn, fruit, vegetables, and jars of preserves. Immediately behind them, navigating the waves on his courageous rock pony, was Guadalupe, the only son of Epimenio and Crespina, born in El Cañón in 1894. He was clad in chaparreras with silver buttons and was driving his fat cattle before him, the herd straining to keep their necks above the foaming water. Behind "Walo" we saw El Conjunto de los Hermanos Chavarría and Don Laureano Moraga and his daughter Teresa. They were laughing and singing and steering their guitars through a whirlpool. They were followed by Don Gaspar, the old man who smoked a pipe and lived in a tree. He was sailing the ancient cottonwood he called home like a seven-masted schooner. Then came the Apache, "Narices Mochas," and his wives, of the Tsé Jiné clan, the compadres of the Salazares. They were buoyant on burlap bags full of their wild harvest of acorns, walnuts, saguaro fruit, mesquite beans, and nopalitos. Following close behind them was Doña Juana Moraga, kneeling in a raft made of her prayer and catechism books; she was dressed primly in a high-necked blouse and long, gray, manta skirt.

The lightning flashed, the thunder exploded. There was no letup in the inundation. We were all silent on the hill, transfixed by the spirits in their phantom barks. José Tapia bobbed by riding a miner's helmet as big as a washtub. His legs were dangling over the sides, his steel-tipped boots were flashing, his face was blackened by the candle soot of his years of labor underground. Next came Doña Chepa Durán and Doña Livoria Castro, the midwives of El Cañón, their apron pockets brimming with herbs — mariola, romero, inmortal, canela, albácar, hierba del lobo, and lechuguilla.[5] They were straddling a tree

[5] herbs used by midwives in birthing

trunk to which they had lashed a clean white sheet; the prow was a teakettle full of boiling water. Juan Martínez, the famous gardener of El Cañón, was swimming next to his vegetable cart: it was listing with its heavy load of chile, corn, onions, beans, peas, tomatoes, garlic, and squash. Then Jesús Macías, the woodcutter, maneuvered through the current, steadying himself on the back of his burro, which was laden with cords of firewood. The trappers, the Rubal brothers, paddled gaily by in hide canoes stitched together of rabbit pelts. And finally came El Padrino Santa Cruz, the godfather of all the children, the saint of El Cañón. The newly baptized children, dressed in hand-stitched, long, white gowns trimmed with crocheted lace, were clambering on his shoulders and hanging in ropes from his outstretched arms. The head of Niño Santa Cruz was backlit in the form of a halo by the lightning. HE WAS WALKING ON THE WATER.

The creek was still cresting. The roar was deafening, the monsoon unremitting. Teodoro Sánchez' mule was snorting and restless. She was skittish and wild-eyed, pawing at the ground. "C'mon," Teodoro told me over the din of the storm. "Hop up on Lola. I can get you out. She can carry us both out of here the back way on the old San Carlos Trail through the Santa Teresa Mountains."

His face was melting in the downpour. I could barely see him: he was a specter himself, fading in the wash of the rain. And yet on the horizon I caught a glimpse of the trailing fringes of a rainbow wrapping itself like a rebozo on the somber and bruised mountains.

"No thanks," I told him gravely, looking at the hills. I looked at the rising creek. The water and the memories were lapping at my feet. My heart was being swept away like a leaf in an eddy. "No thanks. I can't get out. I can never get out."

About the Author

Patricia Preciado Martin is a native Arizonan and lifelong Tucsonense. She is an honors graduate from the University of Arizona and has been active in the Chicano community of Tucson for many years.

Her books include two collections of oral history, *Songs My Mother Sang to Me: An Oral History of Mexican American Women* (1992) and *Images and Conversations: Mexican Americans Recall a Southwestern Past* (1983), both published by the University of Arizona Press. She has written a collection of prize-winning short stories, *Days of Plenty, Days of Want* (1988, Bilingual Review Press), and her work has been included in numerous anthologies.

She lives in Tucson with her husband, Jim, and counts the hours until her children visit.